KING OF FROST

FAE OF DARKNESS

ANA CALIN

ALL RIGHTS RESERVED
No part of this book may be reproduced or transmitted in
any form or by any means, electronic or mechanical, including photocopying, recording, or by any information storage
and retrieval system, without permission in writing from the author except in the case of brief quotations embodied in reviews.
Publisher's Note:
This is a work of fiction,
the work of the author's imagination.
Any resemblance to real persons or events is coincidental.

Copyright January 2020 – Ana Calin

Table of Contents

Title Page 1
Copyright Page 2
CHAPTER I 4
CHAPTER II 25
CHAPTER III 48
CHAPTER IV 58
CHAPTER V... 85
CHAPTER VI 107
CHAPTER VII 120

CHAPTER I

Arielle

HUMILIATION, MOCKERY, that's what this is. The powerful Lord of Winter took everything from me, and now he's pledging himself to another woman, while making me watch.

"It's just an engagement," Edith says, her fingers working on my elaborate hairdo. I watch her pretty reflection in the vanity mirror, her silver hair coiling in braids around her head, framing her heart-shaped face. Her big eyes meet mine against the pane, soft brown on sad blue.

"He's not actually marrying her tonight." She presses her cheek to mine. "It's just the engagement."

"Engaged or married, it's the same commitment between High Fae, and you know it." I mask my pain with anger. "The bond is unbreakable."

I jut out my chin, watching Edith put the sparkling sapphire necklace on my chest, and tying it behind my neck. With my hair braided up in the same fashion as Edith's, I seem to have a swan neck, snow-white skin contrasting with ebony hair.

"You're so beautiful," Edith whispers, "*princess.*"

I smile, a hand on the sapphire necklace.

"Thank you," I manage, but my voice breaks again over repressed tears. What's the point of being beautiful, or a sea fae princess, heiress to the entire power of the oceans, if you can't grasp that power, and you've been chained to a man who makes all decisions in your place.

I push back my chair, its legs scratching the stone. I walk to the arched window, staring out at the wild ocean as it crashes against the castle's rocky base, letting the chill dry my eyes. I breathe in, salty air filling my lungs. The shiny blue corset tightens on my body, but the lower part is made of vaporous folds, weightless as the breeze, allowing the air to caress them like leaves on a tree.

"It was King Lysander himself who had it made for you," Edith says behind me, her fingers working the folds of my dress.

"Another way to state his power over me before he marries another woman."

"It's not definitive, Arielle," Edith insists, making me look at her. "They're not getting married, this is the engagement ball, get that through your head. A lot can happen between now and the wedding."

I whirl around, my dress brushing hers. "You know very well Lysander needs Minerva's military connections in order to gain the advantage over Xerxes. She will pull the rug if he *ever* breaks that commitment. Minerva is many things, especially a total bitch, but she's not an idiot."

Edith's sweet mouth tightens. What can she possibly say, she knows I'm right.

I look down at my arms, the silver drawings shimmering just under my skin.

"Look at me. The ocean king's heiress, trapped in the Lord of Winter's tower by the ocean. He chained my powers, imprisoned me, limited me in every way he could think of, while he takes all the liberties in the world." I scoff bitterly. "He's a manipulative villain. He's got control over my powers, and now he's acquiring Minerva's, too. Killed two birds with one stone."

Edith takes my hand in hers, searching my eyes. "Arielle, King Lysander is not in love with Minerva. He's only doing this for strategic and military reasons. It's you that he has feelings for."

I pull back my hand and walk to the vanity table. "Oh come on, I know him well enough by now. He only loves power."

"Let me remind you that it was Minerva who requested this union, and she did it when Lysander asked for her help in order to ensure *your* safety. When this is over, I'm sure he's also going to restore your full control over your powers. He only chained them because you'd wreak havoc without proper training. You've never wielded such force before, Arielle, you have no idea the chaos and destruction it can cause. You lived your whole life in the mortal world, barely scratching the surface of magic. You had no idea you were the ocean king's sole heiress."

"Water has always called to me," I whisper, staring into the mirror as if it could transport me back in time.

"Every time I was near water, I felt powerful, ecstatic even. If I'd ever been by the ocean, my power might have exploded to the surface, and maybe it would now too, without his silver spell on me. Lysander has no right to separate me from my legacy. He could help me master it. Teach me how to handle the big guns. But no, he wants to keep my power for himself, use me for his own purposes, and don't you even try to defend him, Edith, because you know damn well I'm right. You have a pure heart, you're a romantic and want to believe there's romance at work here, but there's nothing romantic about this situation."

Knocking announces the presence of a guard, his ice-silver mail glimmering in the cold winter sunlight as he stands between the grand double doors. He stares at us for a few moments before he clears his throat and resumes his detached demeanor.

"You are expected in the banquet hall," he announces, and stands to the side. I look to Edith.

"It's time," she whispers, squeezing my hand. "If it's too much to bear, lean on me. We'll get through this together."

I take a deep breath, deciding to fake it until I make it—act cool, composed, dignified. But it won't be easy to watch Lysander pledge himself to another. Actually, I expect it to hurt like hell.

My heart beats faster with every step I take down the grand stairs towards the banquet hall. Silver and ice arches blind us, clamoring and voices flooding the castle, turning louder as we descend into the thick of the crowd. It takes a while until my eyes adjust to the glamour, and I can see people's reactions. Edith squeezes my arm.

"Everybody's staring," I whisper.

"That's because you're incredibly beautiful." I detect enthusiasm behind her words.

"Or maybe they're just curious about the ocean king's only descendant."

Clusters of elegant and dignified attendees move aside as we walk deeper into the hall towards the large archways that open towards the sea, no windows shielding the hall from ocean breeze and the sound of crashing waves. I'm finally able to make out figures and faces against the glamour. We're walking past brown-haired fae dressed in leaf-green robes and tunics that look impeccable. Some wear robes encrusted with precious stones, marking them as high noblemen and ladies of ancient respectable houses.

"Woodland fae," Edith breathes in my ear. "Minerva's family supported them in their campaigns for decades, which is why they feel they have a debt of honor to her. They're one of the reasons Lysander is doing this."

As my sight fully clears I realize there's a myriad of supernatural creatures, all of them even more impressive than in fairy tales. I can barely keep my jaw together, my eyes roaming as Edith and I sweep by them.

There are people with special skin that glimmers like scales in the light—serpent and dragon shifters, the real deal. A minotaur family close to Minerva's silver-and-gold haired clan with their bright silken robes, tunics and gowns, and a group of witches with pointed hats holding goblets of wine on Lysander's side of the hall. There are vampires, too, I can distinguish them by the deathly pallor of their faces, and the blood-red lips. They're as beautiful as the fae, and look as dangerous as the mages. Fascinating creatures.

Also on Lysander's side, a few tall, dark and brooding men accompany the richly bejeweled mages. Warlocks by their sullen demeanor, black suits and intense gazes.

"Oh my God, Zillard Dark is here," Edith says, gripping my arm tightly. Her soft brown eyes are alight, fixed on one of the warlocks, the tallest one.

"Dark Who?"

"Zillard, he's a rising star. Rather young, but very powerful, and especially vicious, they say. He's the son of Hades."

"Hades as in the Lord of Tartarus?"

"The very same."

I glance back to the minotaur family, mythical creature that are fascinating to behold.

I watch Zillard Dark as we head towards the front of the hall. We have spots reserved at a white table close to the crystal dais, and I can barely believe it when I read Edith's and my names right next to Zillard's.

"Oh my God, I can't believe this, doll, he's gonna be sitting with us," Edith giggles. She's so anxious her face has gone crimson.

"You sure seem to know a lot about him. Why the special interest?"

"He goes to the Major Arcana Academy, with Minerva's youngest sister, Giselle. He's a nasty one, everyone has heard about him."

I lock eyes with Zillard Dark as a guard holds my chair out for me to sit. The look in his eyes tells me he knows something, and I'm sure he somehow manipulated our sitting arrangement.

He prowls over like a panther in his black suit, his dark hair slicked back, his eyes black as coals, quite shocking against the backdrop of his skin. He takes his seat by my side with fluid moves, goblet in his hand.

"Daughter of the ocean," he says, his deep voice laced with danger. "An honor to be seated at your table."

"An honor you've ensured yourself, am I right?"

Edith stiffens by my side, but Zillard smiles, revealing white teeth. The canines are longer and sharper than the others. A predator, all right.

"You're a quick woman."

"To what do I owe the pleasure of your company?"

He looks around from under his eyebrows, as if masking something. "Too many curious eyes and ears. In due time."

Guards march in, their armor and weapons clamoring, announcing the festivity is about to begin. I steel myself for the entrance of Lysander and Minerva, but it's old Iridion that takes the stand, dressed in a white robe and leaning on his ivory cane, looking like an angel. An aura of power surrounds him.

"Dearly beloved," he begins. I lick my parched lips, praying for the strength to stand this through with dignity. It will take a miracle. "We have gathered here to bless the engagement vows of our King of the Court of Ice, Lord of the Winter Realm Lysander Nightfrost, and Lady Minerva Midwinter—" He goes on to enumerate Minerva's titles, among which White Lady of the Winter Realm.

"There are rumors that the King is only marrying Minerva for strategic reasons, is that true?" Zillard inquires quietly, taking advantage of everyone's attention being absorbed by old Iridion. I lean in just a little.

"Why do you ask *me* that of all people?"

"Because rumor also says you would have been his first choice for a bride."

Scenarios of what might have been pop up in my head, which makes my heart twist. My throat cords up. "A load of crap. The King only cares about power. So you can tell Minerva she can relax, I'm not her competition."

Zillard must be her guest, and he's having this conversation with me on her behalf. Maybe she sent him to threaten me not to start anything with Lysander.

"Actually, I'm here for King Lysander. My father, he and I have a relative in common."

"You mean to tell me Lysander has hellish blood?"

"I'm afraid you're mixing things up. My father doesn't rule Hell, he rules Tartarus. Many mistake Tartarus and Hell for the same thing, but Tartarus is a higher realm than Hell. It's its outer layer, if you like. And no, Lysander doesn't share the blood."

"Then how can you have a relative in common?"

He grins. "It's complicated."

I keep staring at him, another question popping up in my head. "Wait a minute, if Tartarus is the outer layer of Hell, what does that make the Winter Realm and the Fire Realm?"

"They're the poles. Imagine Hell like a planet, and they keep its balance. Tartarus is like the magnetic field around it."

Silence falls between us, only Iridion's painful words filling the air, praising the union between Lysander and Minerva. Damn it, I'm starting to hyperventilate.

"So, is it true that you met Xerxes Blazeborn in person?" Zillard says, and frankly I'm grateful for the distraction.

"Yes."

He leans in closer, his scent of burnt incense wafting to my nostrils. "Is it also true that, after you escaped the Fire King's trap, you had an affair with the Lord of Winter?"

Embarrassment shoots to my cheeks, but I manage to keep my tone even.

"I told you, those rumors are just a load of crap."

"Yeah, I know, but I'm not talking about rumors here. I have informers."

I remember the Christmas party at the French inn. I don't have to sift very long through my memories to understand who it was. I discovered I have a special magic sense that enables me to judge human character very fast. Too bad it doesn't always work on supernaturals.

"The innkeeper, he seemed a jolly fellow that liked to tell stories. I wouldn't take him too seriously."

"You can twist and turn it all you want, Lady de Saelaria, but I can smell a lie. You've been intimate with the Lord of Winter."

Music floods as hall as the men lining the walls raise their party flags.

Lysander and Minerva step onto a pedestal in fanfare-like music, her hand on his like on a scepter. People burst into applause, white doves and sparkling snow flying into the air. I can't bring myself to stand, my legs just won't listen. My heart hurts so bad it seems to shrivel inside my chest, and my fingers clutch at the folds of my dress.

With the noble fae at the table in front of us standing, clapping heir hands and cheering, I can't get a clear view of the couple, which is a blessing. All I get is glimpses of Minerva's gold and silver hair up in an impressive halo of a chignon, her dress shimmering blindingly. As if it weren't enough that she's a winter fae, she went for so much bling-bling it makes it hard to watch her.

Then, between the figures of the standing supernaturals, I glimpse Lysander, and a dagger runs through my heart.

Everything about him screams 'king', especially his large shoulders, and the beautiful golden hair that flows in wild waves. He's wearing the silver mail that his own flesh transforms into, making him appear to be a statue of liquid metal. His bright blue eyes find me, and for a second it feels like our souls connect. He's remembering our night together, I can feel it as clearly as I do the breeze on my face. He remembers my touch, my mouth crushed to his—

"What if I told you there was someone who could lift his silver spell, and restore your power," Zillard's voice appears inside my mind.

My head snaps to him, but he's not even looking at me. His black eyes are fixed ahead, his lips set. He's using telepathy.

"Are you serious?"

He nods, just slightly. I can feel Lysander's eyes drift from me to Zillard, but the noble fae at the table in front of us shift, and disrupt his field of vision. I reach down into my core, tapping into my telepathic powers.

"Anyone who tries to lift the silver spell that Lysander put on me dies. At least that's what he told me."

"It's true. The only way to break the spell is by killing Lysander, but judging by the way you look at him, I don't think you want that."

Was one glance at Lysander enough to betray my feelings for him? I square my jaw and my shoulders, holding my ground like I don't care, but on the inside I'm giddy as hell.

"I would like to get my power back—it's mine, after all. Lysander had no right to bind it, seal it away somewhere where I can't reach it. But I would never have him killed, even if I could, because I don't want his blood on my hands."

"I wouldn't even dream of suggesting that you have him killed. I don't think you'd find anyone willing to even try anyway. He's one of the most dangerous fae that ever lived. But I know someone who can help you regain control over your powers. A sea creature

with more command of magic than anyone, even Lysander."

"*Who?*" I'm growing dangerously excited. I can already see myself reveling in furious ocean waves, high and deadly, waves that could tear this very castle apart.

"*The sea witch.*"

His words crash into my mind, taking me by surprise.

"I must really look like an idiot to you, Mr. Dark," I hiss through my teeth, raising my eyebrows at the warlock. I don't even know what angers me more, the disappointment because I got my hopes high for a second, or his taking me for a fool. "The sea witch would kill me on sight. She is the one that caused my family's demise."

"And she is the one best suited to restore your rightful powers." He gives me a crooked, cunning smile. "Of course, she will want something in return."

"She. Wants. Me. Dead." I look daggers at him. "Reaching out to her would be like swimming right into the jaws of a shark."

"Look, Arielle, it's been thousands of years since the sea witch wiped out the ocean king's family, and she's still not ruling the seas. She held the Trident for very little time before someone else claimed it. Do you know who runs the seas these days, by the way?"

"I wasn't aware that someone did."

He gives a low laugh. "There can never be order without authority, that's a lesson I suggest you learn fast. The seas would be a boiling warzone if Calabriel Seawrath didn't hold those reins tightly."

"Calabriel Seawrath." I knit my eyebrows. "Who is that?"

"The Steward of the Sea Court. Without a living descendant of the ocean king, the castellan's family overthrew the sea witch and kept the power. He wants nothing more than to be crowned king, but that's impossible." He gives me a quick once-over. "You exist, so the great sea magic never rose to occupy his veins. Still, he commands great armies of merfolk, and would make a great ally against Xerxes. But, as you can see, he wasn't even invited to the engagement ball."

"That sounds extreme, somehow. There must be a grave reason for that."

"There is. Minerva handled the invitations. Calabriel and Minerva have been sleeping together for years."

"They've what?" I yelp in shock, which draws attention. I clear my throat and return to telepathic communication.

"Then why the hell did Minerva demand to have Lysander, if she was already involved with Calabriel?"

Zillard laughs quietly, but seems genuinely amused. *"Calabriel will never have real power, Arielle. He is not the rightful heir of the sea magic, he's from a family of castellans. He'll never acquire real status among supernaturals and, to be honest, Minerva's family would have never accepted the union. Besides, I think she's developing an unhealthy obsession for your Lysander."*

My Lysander. I feel the truth of those words so deeply, that I can't even contest them to save face.

People clap their hands as old Iridion finishes his speech, coiling a silver cloth around the joined hands of Lysander and Minerva. I swallow down the painful knot that scrapes my throat.

Applause explodes from all around, filling the glittery room. Natural earthy and mossy fragrances waft around me, the sea breeze teasing my senses, but I can't enjoy it. Lysander's union with Minerva hurts so much it's hard to breathe. It doesn't help that I feel his eyes on me as the ball continues into the night, flowing music enticing dancers to glide over the marble dance floor.

Thirsty for answers, I look around for Zillard, but he's nowhere to be seen.

I mix with different clusters of fae, meeting people, determined to find him, but I'm only pulled in deeper with the people. The woodland fae seem eager to meet me, some of them even happy, but the shifters and witches keep a suspicious frown on their brow. I can hear them as I pass by, their whispers reaching me like the breath of ghosts.

I hadn't wanted to believe Zillard, but he was right about the rumors. He'd actually gone easy on me. What reaches my ears is a different version— apparently I'm shamelessly chasing Lysander, while he remains completely uninterested; how could the mighty King of the Court of Ice, the Lord of Winter and King of Frost, ever lower his standards to a half-fae of twenty-two years, no matter her heritage. Heiress of the ocean king or not, I'm still a hybrid, half human, and not worthy of the great king, they say.

With clenched teeth, I swear that I'll take my power back from Lysander. I won't let him and his people walk all over me like this.

Finally, I find Edith.

"Edith, please." I take her hands. "Help me find Zillard."

Edith shudders when she hears the name.

"You shouldn't keep his company, doll. He's dangerous. He may seem pleasant to be around, but that's just a façade."

"Façade or not, he told me there was a way for me to regain control of my powers without Lysander."

"Let me guess, it's something dangerous that could get you killed, right?"

"More or less."

"Don't trust him, Arielle." She grabs my hand, her tone urgent. There's fear in her eyes, but also a certain reverence for the dark Zillard. "If he's not even here anymore, it's because he only came here to plant some crazy idea in your head. You can't trust Zillard Dark, or anyone in his family, or his coven, or anyone who knows him and doesn't hate him, for that matter."

"He and Lysander are on good terms. So I guess—"

"King Lysander rules the Other Side of Hell, a realm as dangerous as Hades'. He and the Darks respect each other, but they're not friends, trust me."

I find the strength to lock eyes with Lysander again. As expected, his were already on me. He's sitting at a royally laden table by the high archways, the big bad winter king on his throne of icicles that look like swords. A king as dangerous as Zillard Dark. No better than him.

"There you are, girls." Pablo says, technically slamming into poor Edith. Warmth pools around my heart when I see him.

"Been trying to get to you guys for ages, but with all the woodland folk surrounding you like you're treasure, it was impossible."

"See," Edith says, her pretty brown eyes still heavy with worry. "Everybody here knows you're the descendant of the ocean king, and that you could wield the entire power of the seas. Zillard Dark of all people surely had a hidden agenda with you."

"Zillard Dark?" Pablo shrieks, looking from Edith to me. "He was here?"

His white hair has started to catch strands of silver, now arranged into a carefully disheveled fashion. He's wearing a silver tunic like most winter fae, ornate with golden embellishments. But something sets him apart. He wears dark pants with a special sheen that marks Pablo as more feminine than the rest of the male fae in here. His delicate nerdy-scholar face adds to the girly air, too, which is probably why I get this sister vibe from him.

Three powerful knocks echo through the hall. It's old Iridion, beating his ivory cane against the dais, calling for attention.

"Noble and treasured families, ladies and gentlemen," he begins in a warm old voice. "As you know, we have gathered here for more than engagement vows between two members of powerful lineages, a royal and a high noble. We have gathered here because we're facing a common threat, one that has been around for many thousands of years, but that spins out of control now. You all know this to be true." He pauses to let his eyes sweep over the crowd.

"In the invitation King Lysander and Lady Minerva sent, they didn't keep any secrets," he continues. "They revealed their union comes with military commitment to each other, a commitment against a common enemy—Xerxes Blazeborn, whose wrath threatens to tip the balance between the two sides of Hell, or the two Poles, as most of you know them. He's been waging war against the Winter Realm for many years, but now he's taking it to a new level. It all started when he demanded the ocean king's descendant to be traded over to him—" He motions in my general direction, and so many eyes follow him, that the skin crawls on my arms. "With the intent of making her his mate, and using her power. Now, a combination of their powers would have been deadly not only for the winter fae, but for all of us. We all know that Xerxes is a warmonger, and addicted to power. If King Lysander would have conceded his request, many realms would not even exist anymore.

"But Xerxes still wants Lady Arielle de Saelaria at all costs and, with her power, he plans to take over the human realm. And we all know what that means." Whispers travel through the hall. Worry charges the atmosphere. The Earth is at the center of all layered realms, whoever controls the Earth, controls all the other dimensions. Which is why the Earth is so heavily guarded, and why all supernaturals crossing the border are brutally punished.

Minerva steps forward, and all attention shifts to her.

"Treasured woodland folk, beloved serpent lords, my dear winter folk," she calls, a true ice queen in her glittery dress. I swallow painfully. "The path and destinies of our families have been entwined for many centuries. We fought wars together, and celebrated together, we shared the good, the bad, and the ugly. Strong relations are based on trust and mutual support. My family has never called on you for petty or selfish reasons. You know Xerxes Blazeborn. Some of you have clashed with him more than once, you know how vicious he can be, and how greedy for power. As we speak, he's gathering his allies to move against us, and we have to be ready." She raises a hand in the air, magic crackling in her palm. "Join the Lord of Winter and me on this quest, and let us ensure balance. Xerxes is unstable, he's like a human tyrant with a twitchy finger over the button of a nuke. This threat has been dangling over our heads for far too long, and we've been far too tolerant. No more. Let us put a stop to Xerxes' terror."

The ice lady can sure inspire a crowd, I'll give her that. I didn't even notice how tight my lips were until a mage rises from the back, long robes flowing around him along with his black magic. He has the long haggard face of an evil warlock.

"By virtue of the good ties between your bloodlines and mine, Lady Midwinter, King Nightfrost, allow me to suggest an alternative." His small, bullet-like eyes find me. "If Lady de Saelaria is the apple of discord, then it might be advisable to cut the evil from the root. I know that my idea may sound, how should I say, unconventional, to a certain extent even barbaric, but considering the stakes I'm going to say it anyway—If this problem arose when Lady de Saelaria came into the picture, the problem should cease to exist once she does."

It takes me a few moments to wrap my mind around what he just said, and apparently I'm not the only one having trouble. There's a lag between his last sentence, and the first gasps.

"Excuse me," I finally manage. My hand tightens around the stem of my goblet.

"Please, Lady de Saelaria, don't take this personally. Your sacrifice would be for the greater good."

"The greater good? Really, and that is the only solution you could come up with? Forgive me, Sir, if I doubt your pure, non-personal intentions. You could have suggested that I run away, that I should go into hiding, you could have even intervened on my behalf for the Lord of Winter to unchain my powers, and let me use them to protect myself. Instead, your best idea is to kill me. So, no, sorry, I don't believe you're interested solely in the greater good. You're just in the mood for a legal murder." The warlock's hollow cheeks grow dark red with rage.

Voices rise, ignoring old Iridion's demands for silence. Most people are outraged, but some are considering his proposition as a good alternative. Some become vocal, calling out that it should at least be discussed in the Council.

"Enough," Lysander's voice booms into the hall, sweeping like a rippling wave through the crowd. He instills fear as he rises from his throne, his wavy hair glowing like rivers of gold. "Killing Arielle de Saelaria would only give Xerxes a pretext to attack with all he's got. You're not the first one to come up with that idea, Mage Igarus, I have thought about it myself."

Please tell me he didn't just say that. A black nightmare has eclipsed my heart and clawed its way into my brain. I hitch the folds of my dress and run out of the banquet hall, people moving out of my way.

I storm between the guards, up the grand stairway, tears streaming from my eyes. Finally, I slam the doors to my chamber shut, finding much needed privacy. I can't be around anybody right now, except one person. The only soul that can soothe mine.

"Arielle." It's Edith's voice, muffled from behind the door. "What are you doing? Let me in, unlock the door."

"Don't run away from this fight, we're standing with you." That was Sandros' deep warrior voice.

"We're on your side, Arielle, but you need to be strong and fight this," Pablo adds.

And yet the man that should be on my side, the only man who ever saw me naked, enjoyed my favors, been profoundly intimate with me, has just stated that he'd thought about killing me himself. I press my eyes shut, unable to cope with the memory of his words, of his face as he said it. It blends in well with the first time we met, when he chained me in his ice magic and threw me in a dungeon to freeze to death.

My friends knock harder on my door. Sandros throws his big warrior bulk against the heavy wood in an attempt to break it down, and he'll soon succeed. But when he does, it's too late for me. Just when the door bursts form its locks I step from the window ledge, and into the waves crashing against the castle base.

CHAPTER II

Arielle

The door opens just a little, stopping against the safety chain. Familiar eyes blink at me from behind round glasses.

"By the high realms," she whispers, and the chain falls off. She opens the door widely, allowing me to enter. I walk inside, every step heavy from my weight. My gown is soaking wet, dripping on the floor. My hair clings to my face, Edith's elaborate hairdo destroyed, while my hands tremble, my fingers curled in and painful from the cold.

"H-hello, Auntie," I babble, while Aunt Miriam closes the door behind me. Just as I prepare to explain, she throws her arms around me, bursting into tears.

"My child, my sweet child," she whimpers, cupping my face and rising on the tips of her toes to kiss my cheeks all over. "You're here, by the highest realms, you're here."

She leads me straight into the bathroom, helping me into the bathtub. I go along with everything she does, my body shivering hard, my teeth chattering. I just sit here in the bathtub like a stray dog as Aunt Miriam cuts the gown off of me with big scissors, until

I'm completely naked and bracing my knees to my chest as warm water begins streaming down my back.

Aunt Miriam increases the temperature, thawing my body gradually. It must be over an hour before I finally sit down in my spot at the kitchen table, steaming ginger tea under my nose, my old blanket with unicorns wrapped around my shoulders. Aunt Miriam sits across from me, staring like I'm the crown jewels. Poor woman hasn't heard from me ever since Lysander took me, and his messengers afterwards had been vague regarding my fate.

"How did you get here from the Flipside?" she inquires, caressing me, full of tears.

"I used the only portal I knew how to use—the ocean. I jumped in."

"By the high realms! That could have gotten you killed!"

"I just had to get out of there. I couldn't take, his, his—" I burst into tears, burying my face in my palms.

Aunt Miriam cries with me, taking me in her arms. I can feel her love permeate my soul, and it's what gives me the strength to tell her the story. I only manage a short version, though. Lysander the Lord of Winter discovered I was the ocean king's descendant; first he wanted to trade me over to Xerxes the Fire King, but changed his mind when he realized that Xerxes already had a way in place to trick himself out of his oath never to attack Winter Realm, and would instead use me to bring about the end of the world as we know it; he chained my powers for fear I might lose control over them and wreak havoc, and the only way to free my powers from those chains is to kill him—or go to the sea witch.

"No, you must never," Aunt Miriam reacts as if burnt. "That woman is powerful, and evil, both of them to the extreme. Without your full powers, you won't stand a chance against her."

"The person who told me about this possibility says I might have something she wants, something I can use in order to bargain with her. Maybe I'll be able to strike a deal."

Aunt Miriam needs time to adjust to all of this. So much has happened, and I can tell it's not easy for her to take it, even though she's doing her best not to show that it's affecting her.

"Think about it, Aunt Miriam. The sea witch had all of the ocean king's possible descendants killed, or so she thought, but what good has that done her? She's still not ruling the seas. Now it's someone else she's bitter against."

Aunt Miriam ponders, still stroking my hair.

"I could renounce my title and my reign, allowing her to have both—in exchange for my power."

"Did your so-called 'informer' suggest that?"

"No, it's my idea."

"I think you should at least have a clear discussion with whoever put these things inside your head before you do anything. Remember how dangerous it can be. It might be safer to try and persuade the Lord of Winter. Besides, I hate to say it, but he's right—having full command of your powers without proper training would mean chaos, it could even get you killed. But, on the other hand, he could train you, and restore your powers as you go."

"He could, but he won't, because he's an evil bastard." I push the stool so hard that it crashes against the wall. Aunt Miriam winces, her eyes widening at me as if she can't believe it.

"A few months in the supernatural world, and you already have superhuman strength," she whispers.

"I'm angry, Auntie. Lysander Nightfrost and I aren't on the best terms, so don't rely on his help. He won't do it."

"You're a hard woman to help, Arielle de Saelaria, especially since you keep breaking the law."

That voice. Deep and vibrant. Lysander's voice.

I freeze by the kitchen window, eyes fixed on the irises watching me from the dark corridor. The sharp blue irises of an ice beast. Lysander steps inside, the shadow stripping off of him like a cloak.

How the hell did he know where I was? Did he pick up my trail, followed it to the bottom of the ocean—the portal he himself taught me how to use?

"Do whatever you want with me, but leave Aunt Miriam out of it." I can barely keep my chin from trembling with a mix of fear and anger, my fingers curling into my unicorn blanket.

"Supernaturals speak in favor of your death at the ball, and the next thing you do is go ahead and break the law again? What in the cursed realms were you thinking?" He snarls the question, his lip curling over his perfectly white teeth as he walks closer. His presence fills the room. I look him up and down, still trying to understand how he found me.

He's wearing a tight white shirt that threatens to split open across his bulging biceps, and pants that are just as tight on his legs. He must have grabbed them from some yard on his way here. His hair is still wet from the ocean water.

"How did you manage to use the portal to bring you straight here?" he demands to know.

"I don't know, I just wanted to get away from you. The portal brought me back up in the lake by the campus instead of the ocean."

"So it obeyed your heart's desire. That's the next level of using a portal, someone would have had to teach you."

"No one did."

"Then you're a natural. More reason to be kept under observation."

"You conceited bastard," I hiss. "You would kill me with your own hands, if you didn't still need me, so stop the protector charade. Don't think I don't see behind your plot, Lord of Winter, and remember that you have no right over me."

"If you keep acting like an errant child, Arielle, I will punish you as one," he threatens through his teeth.

"Oh, you're gonna bend me over your knee?"

God, he's so infuriating. Heat explodes all over my body, I burn to defy him. Still, I realize I've walked backwards, and now I'm pressed with my back against the window. He traps me between his powerful arms, his face with his sharp ice king features so close to mine that I can smell the scent of his magic, cold coming off his skin.

My nostrils flare, and tears swell out of my eyes. I can't hold back anymore, all those pent up emotions just pour out of me. Before I know it, I'm beating his chest, screaming at him.

"How could you use me like that, you bastard? You'd already pledged yourself to her, and still you took what I offered. You used me for sex, and then tossed me away."

"You what?" Aunt Miriam reacts from the other side of the room, as if my words just electrocuted her back to life. She approaches slowly, inspecting Lysander's sculptured face, her brow furrowing the closer she comes. "What in the cursed realms happened between the two of you? What is going on here?"

My lips seal. Damn it. Because of my outburst, her heart will break into pieces.

Lysander squares his large shoulders, as if assuming responsibility. "We will tell you. But you should probably have a seat."

Lysander

EMOTIONS MIX IN THE old woman's eyes.

"So you took her away from the mortal world to throw her in a dungeon, then you found out who she was, and you saw better ways to use her. Then you slept with her, too."

"Almost," Arielle says from her seat. She's bracing her knees, embarrassed to have revealed our affair to her aunt, huddled in her unicorn blanket. "We *almost* slept with each other, we didn't go the whole way."

She glances at me, but looks away quickly. "We stopped before, you know, the main thing happened."

"I never intended to take advantage of you, Arielle," I say in a low voice. I want to sound detached, but I can't deny the exalting emotion that fills my chest when I'm around her. An emotion I'll never be able to escape, as much as I want to. "I should have stopped even earlier than I did, but I couldn't. I know it's no excuse, but you were too enticing."

"No, it's no excuse," her aunt intervenes, staring at me through her glasses. I can sense her magic boiling just underneath her skin, but she keeps it in check to avoid provoking me. In the end, she has committed a crime by living in the mortal world, even though she never used her magic here, and she chose to live like an aging human. She even looks like she's over seventy. "Even though Arielle is indeed a naturally powerful sea fae, and exuding attraction comes natural to her even without the special magic that's been passed along her bloodline, you are the Lord of Winter. Also known as the King of Frost. Nothing is supposed to get to you, sure as hell not the luring magic of a water nymph, or a mermaid."

"I want to make it up to Arielle." I look at her again, struggling to keep a grip on my heart. "I will grant you any wish you have, as long as it's not to unchain your power, to set you free or—" All right, here it goes. "Or to be with a man."

The idea of her with another man is unbearable, it's hard to even speak it out.

"You've got a nerve," she hisses, daggers shooting out of her glare.

"It's not personal, Arielle. You know why you cannot give yourself to anybody."

"That means you'll grant me only petty desires, things that don't actually matter."

"No, it can be big things. Like not punishing your aunt for still being in the mortal world, even though the reason she was here in the first place—raising you—no longer stands."

Silence falls between the three of us. Despite sitting huddled by the window, Arielle holds my stare. Anger stains her snow-white face. Her silky black hair appears to shimmer, showing me that her power is rising, ready to explode.

"I'm not afraid of punishment, Lord of Winter," Arielle's aunt says. "But I do believe I would be of more use to you free than in a dungeon."

"Of use?" I frown.

"You say you pledged yourself to Minerva Midwinter because of all the allies her family can bring to fight Xerxes," the woman says, getting up from her seat and heading over to the kettle. The kitchen is small, especially with someone of my size inside, so I have to move out of her way. "But Minerva is a lady of the Winter Realm, she should have activated her connections and influence without you, her king, having to do anything in exchange. I can't tell if what she wants is a chance to win your affections, or just power, but I know she's doing all this for selfish reasons." She sets the kettle, taking down three cups from the cupboard. "I don't know what those reasons are just yet, but I'll tell you this—she's surely keeping aces up in her sleeves, secrets she doesn't tell you about."

"Many of her family's allies were only waiting for a chance to snatch the throne from me, some of her cousins would even have tried to seize the power themselves. They would have even joined Xerxes, thinking foolishly that he would share the power with them if he won the war—sadly, vanity makes some of my nobility *that* stupid. It's why I needed the alliance with Minerva to be rock solid. Through her union with me, her family gains legal succession to the throne. If I lose the throne, they lose it, too." Not to mention that, if I'd refused, Minerva would have used her power and influence to hurt Arielle, but I keep that to myself.

"You are a capable king," Miriam says as she pours tea in cups. "Probably old enough to remember the days when the Court of Ice and the Court of Sea were one. Back in creation times. Maybe you even retain some power over the waters?"

"Very little, and no, I wasn't born until the two realms were separated. Hybrid fae of winter and sea wield some of both, but they're not exceptional in any. Winter and sea fae have tried purposefully mating with each other for years, actually, even though there was no mating bond calling them together. They sought to produce enhanced specimens, but the powers diluted on both sides, instead of improving. The only way to gain real power over the seas is, well, I told you."

"*Borrowing* Arielle's power," Miriam says, calmly. "Or becoming her bonded mate."

When she mentions that, my cheek twitches.

"Let me remind you that I'm very old, King Lysander. I understand things really fast."

By the cursed realms—She knows.

"Then I hope you understand this. When Arielle offered me the use of her powers to battle Xerxes, I made a blood oath to her." I say it quietly, feeling the need to justify myself. "I only found out about the, well, side effects of that blood oath after the events with Xerxes. Old Iridion told me."

Miriam raises her eyebrows over the rims of her glasses, her forehead crinkling.

"So you didn't know at the time you made it?"

I shake my head. "No."

"What the hell are you two talking about?" Arielle whispers, cup of tea between her hands, her eyes swinging between her aunt and me.

"But then your engagement with Minerva Midwinter can only be treachery," Miriam says. "You cannot pledge yourself to another woman, your energies will never mix, it's impossible."

"I know." I move around the room, as much as it allows. I'm too large for it, casting a shadow over the crammed cupboards.

"Then why did you go through with the engagement?"

"For the love of God, are you two saying that Lysander and I are...bonded mates?" Arielle shrieks. She sounds terrified of it, which sparks fire in my frozen blood—she doesn't want our bond, and it feels like a dagger being plunged between my ribs.

"I went through with it because I had to, I needed the alliance for all the reasons I told you," I reply to

Miriam, then I look to Arielle. "I want you to know I didn't bind you to me on purpose. I never wanted to force this mates' bond on you."

A faint line appears between her eyebrows. "But aren't mates supposed to be connected from birth? I have even heard versions about supernaturals' soul energy being connected since the souls of two people came into existences, billions of years ago."

"That's true, but High Fae of the highest supernatural bloodline, like you and me, have the liberty of choosing their mates, because of our positions of authority."

"What does that mean?"

"As king of the primordial Court of Ice, I have the freedom of choosing my mate. As descendant of the ocean king, you have the same freedom. Under normal circumstances, the choice is made official through a pledging ritual like you saw at the castle between Minerva and me. Except that this particular ritual was a fraud, because I had already, unknowingly, pledged myself to another." For a moment I allow all the madness I feel to channel towards her through my gaze. "Arielle, when I declared myself willing to die with you, you and I become mated."

A heavy silence fills the space between us. I can feel it spread beyond these walls, over the apartment buildings, stretching out to the brownstone streets towards the campus that Arielle used to go to.

The old woman keeps her eyes on her niece, focused to help her through this. She got over the surprise, and now I get the feeling she actually likes the idea.

"So, let's see if I have this straight," Arielle says. "I no longer have the freedom of choosing my mate. I'm bound to you, and there's no way out of it."

My lips tighten, and my fingers curl into a fist. Jealousy starts to burn in my stomach.

"You would have preferred someone else? Got anyone particular in mind?"

"That's not the point."

"The mating of our souls came along with the blood oath. I repeat, I didn't know it would do this to us."

"What about your fiancée," old Miriam inquires in a patient tone. "She must have a fated mate, and she must know who it is—fae know about their mates their entire lives, long before they meet them. Betraying her fated mate should deeply disturb the balance of her magic."

"Minerva is High Fae as well, so she also has the freedom to choose."

"But she must sense that the ritual didn't work," Miriam says. "Once a mating bond is created, you feel an irresistible pull towards your mate, you know where they are at all times, and when you're around them you're highly charged. She must notice all this."

"So that's how you knew where I was," Arielle whispers. "You sensed me through our bond. But—" She looks to her aunt. "How come I don't sense him?"

That hits me right in the gut. I want her to feel me the way I feel her, but something must have happened during the blood oath that made it much stronger on my side.

"What *do* you feel?" I ask on impulse, sounding more aggressive than I intended. Arielle scans me up and down with that look in her eyes that promises she'll never forgive me, much less love me, at least not willingly. She raises her chin, locking her arms across her chest. She seems to be battling with herself to say it, and when she finally does, it's with defiance.

"I feel attracted to you. After what happened between us in the mountains, I imagine there's no point in denying it. What changed is that now I'm not only always aware of you, but I can also sense it when you're watching me—I felt it at the engagement ball, which was pretty awkward considering you were just pledging yourself to another woman. But I can't sense where you are, or track you down."

"Maybe that's because when I made the blood oath to you, I gave you my blood, but I didn't get yours in return," I say, struggling with my need to grab her and force her to kiss me. "Maybe that's why our feelings for each other are out of balance."

"But now you understand why he pledged himself to another woman, Arielle," her aunt chimes in. "Besides, considering you were already mated, it was impossible for him to resist you in the mountains."

As Arielle falls into silence, her cheeks still burning, I assess Miriam.

"Why do I get the feeling you're on my side here?"

"You are the Lord of Winter, one of the most powerful supernaturals in the world. I can't think of a better mate for my niece, to be perfectly honest. Besides, you're mated now, so what's done is done. Better make the best of it."

"There has to be a way out if it," Arielle bursts out. "I can't be bound to him forever. He's going to marry someone else, for Christ's sake."

"Sorry to disappoint, but there's no way to break a blood oath." I almost snarl that at her, that's how badly I want it to get inside her head that she'll never be free of me. "Otherwise why would I do everything I did to obtain a blood oath from Xerxes?"

"You said the silver spell that chains my powers cannot be broken either, but it can. Maybe it's the same with the blood oath."

That gives me pause. "Who told you the silver spell can be broken?" Anger seeps into my irises, I can feel ice lighting them up.

"Zillard Dark." She throws the name into my face. That demon, of all people...

"And what exactly did he tell you?"

"That doesn't matter. What matters is that you lied to me. There are ways to break what you did to me. Who knows what else you lied to me about."

"I never lied to you, and I repeat—there is no way to break the blood oath except if I lift it, or if I die."

"All right, the two of you have a lot to set straight, but right now we have more pressing matters," Miriam intervenes. "Xerxes is still after you, Arielle, and he won't stop until he gets you. You need to focus on annihilating that threat. Everything else can wait—even your wedding to Minerva Midwinter, Lord Lysander. I will help you in whatever way I can."

Every ally is important, so I automatically think in what ways she could be useful. A few seconds of scanning her family history in my memory does it.

"Lady Miriam, your father a creature of the underworld, am I right?"

She nods. The subject seems to upset her.

"Descendant of a fallen angel, some old accounts say," I continue.

"Like you said, he was a creature of the underworld."

"And what was he doing in the human realm when he met your mother?"

"Let's just say he was too well known in his own realm, and here he could enjoy some measure of anonymity."

"There are rumors that you inherited a special skill from him."

Her lips draw in a hard line, her eyes flicking to Arielle.

"In all these years," I say quietly, understanding, "you never told her?"

"I think it's better if we discuss this in private."

"No, we're discussing here and now. Arielle an important partaker in this war, she deserves to know everything."

Miriam shakes her head, and it feels like she begs me not to do this. Not to expose her secret to Arielle. But there's no way around it, not anymore.

Lysander

ARIELLE KEEPS LOOKING at her aunt as if struck by lightning. I guess it's not every day that you find out the woman who raised you as a mother has a secret darker than the underworld.

"Your mother's second husband," Arielle whispers. "Your father. He was... He could do all that?"

"He was a creature of the dark. I suppose it comes with the territory," Miriam replies quietly.

"Did grandma know when she married him?"

"What my mother did was a matter of survival," Miriam says. "She needed protection. In the end, being with him became a living hell, and she preferred to fade away and die after a few years, but in the beginning she desperately needed him."

I narrow my eyes, going through Miriam's story in my mind. I heard and read accounts about her mother's second husband, a man of a mysterious and dark bloodline. There was evil in his blood, and Miriam clearly inherited at least some of it.

"Now you might be able to change destiny, Lady Miriam. You can use that power to help us against Xerxes. Put that power in the service of the light."

"It's dark magic, Milord, magic that I haven't used in a very long time," she says, pleading eyes on Arielle, like she desperately wants her niece to understand. "I only did a few times when I was very young, with no real idea what I was doing. When I finally got the harm I was causing around myself—"

"But if you put that skill in the service of our cause, you could make up for all of that. You would be doing something your father was never able to do, namely use it for a good thing," I interrupt, hoping that would help Arielle not to judge her aunt, but rather to see her dark talent as something positive. All dark things can be turned in favor of the good. "Your power might even enable me to back down from the arrangement with Minerva."

The woman smiles. Arielle keeps looking at us intensely.

"But remember the main reason you're doing it is for Arielle's safety," I say gently. "You would make a highly valuable secret weapon. I know you had other ways to help us in mind, you never thought I would require this of you, but think about it. No one would ever see that kind of magic coming, especially not from someone like you."

"I can't use it myself," she says. "I wouldn't survive it." She looks to Arielle with regret. "You will have to take over the burden, my love."

"I'll take the black magic from you, if that's what you want," I say.

"No," Miriam counters. "The only person I'll ever will it to is Arielle."

"But it could do irreparable damage to her."

Miriam places her hand on mine.

"Power comes with responsibility and danger, and sooner or later Arielle will be forced to deal with all that. Besides, she's in more danger without her magic. You won't be able to protect her forever."

"Yes, I will."

"You can't be with her every waking second, King Lysander. She needs her independence, and it's paramount that she gets it soon, as much as the idea frightens you. Besides, you'll soon be married to Minerva, and you'll be even less able to watch over her."

Her old face grows determined, making it clear she's made her decision, and won't be talked out of it.

"Beware, child," she tells Arielle, rising slowly from her chair, her old bones crackling. "You will feel a heavy darkness inside of you, it will spread to all your organs like tar, and it will feel like a black octopus strangling you from inside out. It will be the worst thing you've ever lived through, but when you think you can't take it anymore, remember this— you're becoming a dark fae, but one so powerful it would make Hell seal its gates to keep you out."

She lifts her face to the ceiling as she speaks, spreading out her arms, her words transforming into chanting. Instinctively, I shield Arielle behind me.

"Don't do that, Ice King," Miriam chants, her aura now glowing pale blue, like Caribbean waters, waves rippling through it. "I need her chest bare. Remember why you're doing this."

Her aura shines brighter, now surely visible from the outside like a blast of light. Arielle places herself in front of me, the crown of her head at the level of my chest. I breathe in her scent of sea and fresh linen, the perfume of her silky hair. By the cursed realms, it fills me with emotions so strong they're almost scary.

Darkness seeps like tiny rivulets into Miriam's aura, spreading like ink through crystal-clear waves. Black magic that stains her sea fae glow, but also infuses it with a magic signature that seems forged in the cauldrons of Hell.

My big hands tighten protectively on Arielle's small round shoulders, my jaw tight to keep myself from springing in front of her. I start a chant of my own, deep in my chest, which must be nothing but a low rumble to Arielle's ears. It's a protection spell that I'm ready to cast over her, because I can't risk anything going wrong and hurting her. The protective magic would billow into the air and shield us like a dome of gas-like crystal if things turn nasty.

"No, don't," Arielle shrieks, realizing what I'm doing. She pushes her back into my chest, as if wanting to get me out of her aunt's cluttered kitchen. If humans were in the apartment with us, they would be crushed under the magic pent up here.

Bubbles of murky blue split from Miriam's aura, floating toward Arielle. Ghostly whispers accompany them, the room filling with a skin-crawling sensation that only hellish magic can bring with it. Miriam looks down from the ceiling.

Her face is no longer that of a human old woman. Her irises shine golden, the slit pupils of snake cutting through them. Her now jet black hair floats around her head like the serpents of Medusa. My warrior instincts flare, and it's all I can do not to call forth the sharpest blade of ice, and slice the woman's head off her shoulders.

"Bare your chest for the black snake's nest, oh Pure one," the woman chants, her voice spectral, like a demon's. Arielle's fingers lace through mine, her arm across her chest, shielding her heart.

"You can back out of this, if you want, just say the word," I whisper in her ear, my teeth clenched, all my muscles flexed. I'm ready to step in. It would take only a split second to shield her behind me, and expose myself to the bubbles of infected hell magic, letting them infuse me instead of her.

By the cursed realms, I'd be willing to die for her, right here, right now. In this instant I realize that my only reason for breath is to keep her alive.

"No," the woman shrieks, her whole frame shimmering. She levitates in the air with her arms spread, her terrible snake-like eyes on us. "It has to be her."

"I'll do it," Arielle calls, and removes her hand slowly from mine, thereby removing the barrier across her chest. I can feel the fear in her veins, and it hurts. I want to do something, protect her.

Miriam's chanting fills the room with the energy radiating from her rippling aura.

Open your veins, hand over the reins,
Oh Pure One
It becomes your blood, the snake of hell mud,
Oh Pure One
Raise the blade of power, when night strikes the hour,
Oh Pure One.

The bubbles float around Arielle, forming a ring of hell ink. When the last one joins, they flash into her chest like blades. Arielle crashes against my chest at the impact.

I catch her in my arms and turn her around hastily, cupping her face.

"Take it in, Arielle, don't fight it," I say with all the calm I can muster, my lips close to hers. It cost me great effort not to block the black magic with my blade when it slammed into her, and it's just as hard to control myself now, seeing her eyes rolled back, white foam beading at the corners of her mouth. But now that the magic is inside her body there's no going back, she has to integrate it, or she'll suffer irreparable damage. She shakes hard.

"Your own natural magic is trying to fight off the new one like it's a virus. It's similar to an allergic reaction, and it's usually healthy, but not this time. You have to push through it, force your barriers down."

The shuddering slows, and her eyes roll back to normal, but her blue irises betray she's still not fully here. She looks through me, but I can sense my closeness is helping her. I come down on one knee and lay her over my thigh, one arm under the nape of her neck, cradling her like a child. Her shiny black hair falls over my forearm like a thick blanket of silk, her skin burning.

"I'm not feeling well, Lysander," she manages through white lips.

"What you're going through is normal, the pain will subside in a minute."

I keep talking to her, my words soothing her, as I caress her smooth forehead with my fingers. I can feel her body accept the new magic, quicker than expected, following my guidance. It's a balm to my heart to feel her trust. A thud on the floor makes my eyes dart in its direction, finding Miriam collapsed on the floor.

"I'll be right back," I tell Arielle, and lay her gently on the floor. She sits up, taking a hand to her dizzy head, her limbs still trembling in the aftershocks of pain.

A pool of white spreads around Miriam's head, the first sign she's once again an old human woman. But when I turn her around, I find her pruned like a fig. By the cursed realms. Transferring her secret power to Arielle has caused Miriam's body to weaken even more, and accelerated the aging process. She lies in a thin layer of bluish liquid, which has spilled from her aura, now free of any traces of black.

The woman opens her eyes slowly.

"It's done." She sounds exhausted. "Arielle has my power, but she will need help. You mustn't leave her alone in this, Lord of Winter, whatever happens."

"I'll help her through it, I'll be by her side the whole way," I assure the woman, my arms strong under her weak old body. She feels light as cardboard.

"She'll need your guidance will all her powers," the woman manages. Her words are barely intelligible beyond the wheeze of her lungs. "With her sea magic most of all. It's the most tremendous magic in her veins. Teach her how to fight, too. As the only descendant of the ocean king, and heiress to all his power, she'll have so many enemies she'll lose count." She grimaces in pain, and when she speaks again, I know it's her heart that aches. "She's only a child. Barely twenty-two. Half human. Innocent, as fragile as a fairy, despite powers."

"I will protect her at all times, I promise."

"No, that's not enough. Swear to me that you'll instruct her. Teach her how to use her powers as weapons."

"That would make *her* an uncontrollable weapon, dangerous even to herself."

"Listen." She grabs my forearm and squeezes, but I can barely feel it, she's so weak. "I understand that you want to protect her, but think about it this way. What if you die in a fight? You may be one of the most dangerous and powerful supernaturals in the world, the ancient ruler of the Court of Ice, but your enemies are powerful, too. Even if they don't kill you, it would be enough to separate you from Arielle for a day or two for one of her own antagonists to finish her."

Scenarios flash in my head, and they're all poison. A bitter taste floods my mouth.

"I promise. But that doesn't mean you get to die on us." I scoop her up, and rise to my feet. "Arielle, quickly. A mirror."

CHAPTER III

Arielle

The dark whirl of the portal spits us out at the castle, through an ice mirror in the Council tower. I have just one memory from this place—the day they put me through the test, and threw me into the waves that crash against the castle base. A test that could have killed me.

"Get Iridion, quickly," Lysander commands the guards. He lays Aunt Miriam on the ice Council table.

"Is she going to make it?" I grab the table edges as Lysander runs his hands over her feeble body.

"I have healing magic, but this is a special situation," he replies, moving his hands along Miriam's body like skilled scanners. I remember how he taught me to heal Edith months ago. "The magic she transferred to you was linked to her life force, which is draining rapidly."

The doors bang against the walls, and Iridion storms inside, his ivory cane knocking against the ground. His silver-white hair stands on end, his white robe rippling around him. He's moving faster than I would have thought his old frame capable of.

"Stand aside, Milord," he urges Lysander, yet not without respect. The large king moves out of the way, his ice-blue eyes finding mine.

Old Iridion's spells and magic fade into the background as Lysander lose ourselves in each other's gaze. My heart beats in my throat as his intensity enwraps me. It's the first time I've met his gaze directly after the mountains. I let the connection unfold, searching for the feel of our bond.

Problem is, I've always found him compellingly attractive, on all levels, so I don't know if what I feel now is due to the bond, or if it's just a natural development of that attraction. But no, the chemistry is too strong. In only a few moments, the charge between us exhausts me, especially knowing that I can't have him. My body and soul are aching for his embrace, for his beautiful lips pressed against mine, and that ache weakens me.

"Well, well, well, look what the cat dragged in," a shrill voice resounds against the walls. I turn on my heel, my mouth pressing in a bitter line when I see Minerva. She walks confidently into the hall, like the queen she's about to become, her crimson cape billowing behind her. I remember that Lysander pledged himself to her, and anger returns to the pit of my stomach.

She's wearing an intricately ornate red dress, which accentuates her slim, elegant frame, but her face is just as pointy and unpleasant as ever. And damn, if she would at least quit on that red lipstick, it makes the expression of her mouth even harder than in natural state.

"The little oppressed sea princess is back."

Her jealousy poisons the air, I'm sure even the guards can feel it by the way they watch her. She walks to Lysander, but glares at me like she could ram an iron dagger straight into my throat.

"What took you so long?" she addresses him with false sweetness as her hand snakes around his bicep. "And what in the cursed realms happened with this one?" She creases her nose as she looks down at Miriam, raising an eyebrow.

"She tried to escape when I said I'd take her into custody. This is the result."

"You wanted to take her into custody?" Minerva frowns skeptically.

"It was about time she got hers for staying with the humans, don't you think? Anyway, she won't survive the dungeon in this state. She will receive a room in the castle, and Iridion will keep an eye on her health." He meets my eyes, silently beckoning me to back him up on this.

Minerva squares her bony shoulders. "Well, now that that is taken care of, we have to be on our way soon. Best we leave later today. The Seelie Fae expect us on the Flipside of Scotland tomorrow. If my sources, are right, Xerxes is gathering his own armies, and his fire magic has already started to pierce the veil to the human world."

Lysander's irises flash.

"How do you know that?"

"I told her." That voice. I know it.

And sure enough, Zillard Dark is standing in the doorframe. He's wearing a sleek black suit that's fitted to his body, his black eyes like molten coals.

"It's urgent that we have a word, Lord of Winter," he addresses Lysander. "In private."

"Not in private," Lysander retorts. He keeps his voice commanding, controlled, but so obviously contemptuous of Zillard that I'm sure no one in the room misses it. "Minerva will be joining us, of course, as my pledged future queen, and trusted partner." He addresses the guards. "Announce Sandros." Then he looks at me, an intense secret in his gaze. "Lady Arielle de Saelaria will be joining us as well. I hear that you've already met each other at the engagement ball, so I won't be wasting time with introductions."

Not even a muscle moves on Zillard's face, but he must be mad. He surely expected me to keep the secret from Lysander, which means I've just lost a potentially powerful ally. And which might be exactly what Lysander wanted.

Lysander and Minerva start towards the door, guards trailing after them, while I hover behind, worried about Aunt Miriam. She already started to regain the healthy color of her skin.

"Go in peace, child," Iridion whispers with closed eyes, still immersed in his healing magic that feels like soft winter chill. "When you see her again, she'll be as good as new." He glances at me with glassy, but kind eyes. "I promise you."

Arielle

"WILDFIRES STARTED TO spread in isolated regions in the human world," Zillard reports, sitting back in a silk-cushioned chair with a high back-rest made of beautifully woven wrought silver. We're in the antechamber to Lord Lysander's private apartment where he holds his secret meetings.

"That's how we know where he concentrated most of his fire warriors on the Flipside, but some of these fires could also be decoys, keeping us away from the areas where his real bases are located. I understand he has powerful allies, too."

Lysander stares at him as he speaks like a warlord made of ice and metal. He's so beautiful, it's hard to keep my eyes off of him, but I have to look away if I want to ease the tension in my stomach. When we look at each other, the bond between us activates like charged wires, and we can't risk the others noticing.

Especially not Minerva.

"We can even expect demons, and dragon lords," Sandros says. "He's the Fire Lord, he has special ties with them."

"Demons and dragon lords wouldn't join him, at least not until it looks like he's winning the war," Lysander says. He takes this with impossible calm, the way only an experienced warlord could. "Demons wouldn't jeopardize the balance between the two poles of Hell, it would take centuries to get Lucifer to authorize that. And dragon lords are too proud and vain to come to anyone's aid. They expect to be served, not called on like vassals."

Zillard scoffs. "That still doesn't mean we shouldn't be worrying. The Fire King is resourceful, he surely has serious back-up to start this war."

"I'm sure he's secures support as we speak, I just don't think it's demons and dragon lords." His icy gaze pierces Zillard's stony stare. "He could, for example, be relying on his old friends, the black mages and dark warlocks. You're a member of the Dark Warlocks Order, if I remember correctly?"

"Lysander," Minerva intervenes, "Zillard is here to help. He's not the enemy."

"Isn't he? By the way, did you invite him to our engagement ball, Minerva, because I don't remember putting him on the list."

She hesitates for a moment. "No, I didn't invite him."

"Someone must have, though." Suspicion shadows Lysander's face, enhancing his deliciously dangerous aura. "Strange thing is, he told Arielle he was there on *my* part."

Tension fills the room, hostility sprouting in the air.

"In fact, Zillard Dark was only there long enough to advise Arielle to go and see the sea witch," Lysander continues. "Who is supposedly able to lift the silver spell I put on her to bind her sea powers, powers that could overwhelm her. Now, you both know—" He addresses Minerva and Sandros, "that even if it were true, seeing the sea witch would mean certain death for Arielle."

"It was me who invited Zillard," Sandros speaks up, surprising everyone. The big warrior looks down at his dagger as he plays it in his big hands. His wild dark hair falls over his thick mailed shoulders, his voice rough. "I have relations to black mages and dark warlocks, too. I'm half fire fae, after all."

"I didn't mean to send Arielle to death," Zillard hurries to add. "I just pointed out that there was another way to recover her powers."

Lysander's stare could crush the warlock, but I speak up before he can say anything.

"What if I can help you get Calanbriel Seawrath as an ally?" I say. All faces turn to me, Minerva particularly outraged. She raises an eyebrow, her red mouth twisting in an ugly expression.

"How can a half-fae with the powers of a jelly fish have any influence on Calabriel?" she bites.

"I'm the ocean king's descendant, that should carry some weight, especially in Calabriel's eyes," I counter. "Besides, he didn't honor your engagement ball, I doubt you have other ways of persuading him."

Minerva's face distorts in a mixture of contempt and hatred, but her mouth stays closed. I grin, letting her understand I know about her old affair with him. I wonder if Lysander knows.

"Arielle is joining us to meet our potential allies," Lysander decrees. "Many may be inspired by the only descendant of the ocean king."

Minerva's eyes bulge at him like he's crazy.

"Have you lost your senses? She'll be a burden, she can't even protect herself."

Lysander takes a deep breath, closing his eyes as if to calm himself. When he looks at her again it's with kindness. He wraps his hand around hers and takes it to his cheek, speaking softly to her.

"You and I are pledged to each other now, Minerva, not only to become husband and wife, but also rulers of the Winter Realm together. We're strong enough to get woodland fae on our side, shifters, mages and Seelie Fae. But Xerxes is gathering allies as well, and the forces of darkness are to be reckoned with. Arielle can get us one of the fae leaders that neither of us has particularly strong ties with—Calabriel Seawrath. Maybe she can have an influence on others, too."

His deep, soft voice, the way he gazes at her, the way he holds her hand, all of it goes like a dagger through my heart. He doesn't express love, but warmth and companionship. He's not lying to her or pretending, he just displays all the years they've known each other, and it's enough to make her weak at the knees, I can tell.

Minerva stares at him as if mesmerized, and it tears my guts. She might not have been in love with Lysander when I first met her, even though I did sense her lust for him, but now she's falling, hard.

I jump from my seat and stomp to the window, my guts twisting inside of me in rage and jealousy. What if he's playing the same game with me? What if he's using both Minerva and me through his power of seduction? The bastard is a block of ice, his heart must be as frozen as the darkest depths of the universe. I must resist this magnetic pull he has on me no matter what, in order to save my dignity.

"If Calabriel proves hard to persuade, I could offer him the throne of the Sea Court. Renounce my claim as sole descendant and heiress of the ocean king."

"You would do that?" Sandros whispers behind me, surprised.

"Yes. I'm not interested in political power, Sandros. I just want my sea magic, because I feel it was always part of me, and I have a kind of biological claim on it. Anyway, depending on Calabriel's reaction, which I suspect will be positive, we can decide what to do next."

"We?" Minerva repeats in a mocking tone. "You're not part of the command, half-breed. Of the ancient Sea Court bloodline or not, you'll never be more than a half-fae with the mediocre powers of a water nymph. Don't forget that. Besides, if you expect me to believe you don't the scepter of the Sea Court, you're crazy."

Rage bubbles in my stomach. I grip the ledge of the open archway, closing my eyes to the cold embrace of the setting winter sun, and drawing in a deep breath. When I've regained enough calm to face her without wanting to tear her apart, I turn, slowly.

"I may be a half-breed, a simple water nymph, and whatever else you want to call me, but I'm not stupid. That kind of power comes with responsibility that has proven too much even for ancient fae. I mean, not even the sea witch could hold on to it. What I want, when this is over, is to be free of Xerxes, or anyone who might seek to enslave me for my powers. When this is over..." I jut out my chin, stating my ultimate desire. "I want the freedom to choose a place to live on the Flipside, far away from all of you. I want to be allowed command of at least a part of my powers, and receive guidance to learn magic in depth. I will make a life far away from here, and we never have to see each other again. I'd also like you to help keep my identity secret. I don't want any more greedy supernaturals hunting me down. I'll spend the rest of my life in peace, with Aunt Miriam and, if they'll choose to come along, Edith and Pablo."

Sandros scowls from under his thick dark eyebrows. He's been treating Edith like some kind of personal assistant these past few days, and I suppose he doesn't want to lose her. But even though she owes him her life, it doesn't mean he gets to treat her that way. I will negotiate as hard as I have to for her.

"What if I can help you get what you TRULY want?" the dark voice of Zillard speaks in my mind. I cock my head to the side, but I try not to make it obvious. I don't want the others to know I've gained full control of my telepathic abilities.

"I meant what I said. My desires are simple."

"Trust me, you want to hear me out."

CHAPTER IV

Lysander

Arielle is keeping something from me. She's been suspiciously quiet during the preparations, and on our way here as well. She kept evading me like a ghost through the Seelie King's castle hallways, shrouded in shadow. The magical creatures strolling around often function like a shield for her, and I can't follow when she disappears among them, since I have Minerva on my arm all the time. This being a diplomatic mission, we have to present ourselves together everywhere.

I couldn't resist, and had people follow Arielle, but always in the castle gardens, shadow envelops her. When my scouts make it through, she's gone. It drives me insane, not knowing what she's doing, and with whom—even though I have a hunch there.

At least I know nothing evil can penetrate the secured gates of the Seelie Realm, and hurt her. The only way to access it is through the magical stones in the mortal world, the stones the existence of which has remained a mystery to humans for so long. They lead to supernatural realms, and their gates open only at certain times of day, on specific dates, and only under very special circumstances.

The Flipside of Scotland is filled with primordial magic, and Arielle relishes in it, more than I've ever seen her enjoy anything before. Except maybe my body back in the French mountains. The memory alone hurts, knowing I might never have her again. She has barely even looked at me these past few days, which makes it hard for me to focus on my negotiations with the Seelie King—an old friend, but also a tough negotiator; always trying to trick his way to the best deal possible.

Not to mention that Minerva's advances are getting more difficult to avoid. I made arrangements not to share a chamber with her, invoking that we owe respect to the Seelie Court and won't reside in the same chambers until we are united in proper marriage, but she's teeming with lust.

To be frank, it's no surprise when the door to my room opens. I see her reflection against the windowpane, the robe draped around her shoulders, her gold and silver hair cascading in rings over her bony frame. Her eyes are filled with pent up lust that turned to greed. A greed that reaches down to one's core, a need to own the other or be owned by them. The way I crave to own Arielle.

"Minerva." I keep my posture stiff as I turn to face her, my tone slightly forbidding. She closes the door, the white wood snaking into the locks. She walks over slowly, her naked feet flicking from under the flowing robe with every step she takes. By the way she keeps the sides gathered in front of her chest, she must be naked underneath. There's provocation in the way she looks at me. I raise my chin, hoping to dissuade her from letting the garment pool at her feet and reveal her naked body to me. It's easy to see that's what she intends to do.

"I thought you'd like some company tonight, someone to help you wind down. It's been an intense few days."

"And the next will be at least as demanding. We need to rest."

She smiles, and closes the space between us until she's too close for comfort. "Travel through caves and stone portals for a whole day, then two more negotiating with the Seelie King, you must be tense as a bow. Let me help you with that."

She raises her hand to stroke my jaw, but I catch her wrist. I keep a gentle grip as I lower it. I have to be careful with her, lest she realizes I'm too full of passion for another woman to even see her as one anymore.

"What would help me relax is a good night of solitude, and meditation. I need to feed my powerhouse. We all do," I remind her.

She clicks her tongue, measures me up and down, and starts a slow prowl around me. She runs a finger across my back as she walks, which I'm sure she means as a seductive gesture.

"You and I have known each other for many, many years, Lysander. I'm sure you've known how I feel about you for at least a while now."

Luckily, she's behind me when she says those last words, so she can't see me grimace. She means to sound seductive, but to me, she sounds like a viper.

Which is another strange development since I met Arielle. It's not like I don't enjoy sex. I always did, even though I've also always been careful about my choices, since many of those women were only seduced by my power, status or my looks. I know that Minerva is seduced by all three.

I remain cold as ice, no part of me reacting. I keep searching for that familiar sensation of arousal, if only to convince myself that I can still feel it, but it's not there. Which must be another implication of the mates' bond. My body is as loyal to Arielle as my spirit is, a fact that worries me. It's paramount that I remain master of my feelings, keep the same unshakable control I've always had. I can't let my craving for Arielle take over me.

Minerva has closed her full circle around me, and we now face each other again, her eyes full of provocation. She pushes the gown off her shoulders, and there she is, standing naked in front of me.

I was afraid of that.

"I've always desired you," she slurs, pinching her pointy nipples, and arching her back slightly towards me. "But you were the King. The Lord of Winter who's seen it all in all the years he'd dwelt in the realms. All the women I knew dreamed of one day becoming your chosen one. But we all knew you would only settle for someone who would help further your power and status. You would only marry a woman who meant good business." She licks her upper lip, her look telling. "But luckily the time has come that I'm fantastic business for you."

She pushes her index finger into her mouth, the other hand lowering between her legs. I follow her hand with my eyes as it slips through the blonde fuzz covering the most intimate part of her body, thinking I should give it a try. I should sleep with Minerva. It would put her suspicions to rest, and it would get me off. Hell knows I'm a gunload of pent up sexual energy because of Arielle.

But it doesn't work. I remain cold as ice as Minerva is doing her best to turn me on. My bond to Arielle is even stronger than I thought. I may have put her in chains, but I'm the one who ended up enthralled by her.

I take in the sight of Minerva's nakedness, trying to force arousal, but it just won't work. As much as I let my eyes roam all over her slim, athletic frame, nothing happens, my cock doesn't even twitch inside my pants.

Her eyes narrow. "Am I doing something wrong?"

"There's a lot on my mind, I told you. It's the reason I wanted to avoid this, my mind won't stop working, planning the upcoming meeting with Calabriel. Plus, I like the idea of waiting until the wedding. I like the traditional."

"Like hell you do. I'm not stupid, Lysander. The most prominent thing on your mind is the water nymph. Arielle."

"That's preposterous."

"It's the truth." She picks up her robe and drapes it around her shoulders. "I saw the way you look at her, Lysander. Everybody has. By the cursed realms, it's difficult not to." Anger hardens the lines of her face.

"It's not exactly comfortable for a woman, you know, especially one of my standing, to see her fiancé drooling over another like that."

"It's all just in your head, Minerva." I step closer, and force myself to cup her face in my hands. I run my thumbs over her sharp cheekbones, using a low, grave voice. "Your observation is deep, and quite accurate—marriage must be a worthwhile alliance for me. I would never consider marriage with Arielle, but the only way to gain control over her powers is to play on her feelings. If I control her heart, I control her actions."

Minerva's face relaxes, as if this is exactly what she wanted to hear. She places her hand over mine, her long fingers stroking the back of my hand.

"That gives me relief. But tell me something, Lysander. Besides my connections, my power, my family ramifications, is there anything else that attracts you to me? I ask because, quite frankly, I felt alone in my desire for you all these years. And don't tell me you never noticed I had feelings for you, because we're not children. You've always known."

"Did I look at anyone else the way you would have wanted me to look at you?"

"No. Not until Arielle."

"I told you—I need Arielle to believe I'm into her. She lived her whole life in the human world, and that is how love-sick human men stare at the objects of their desire. That's the language she understands."

Minerva relaxes into my arms that close loosely around her. It's a struggle for me to accept her closeness. My body chemistry simply rejects any woman who isn't Arielle.

"Minerva, once we are married I will have Iridion make one of his famous love potions for us. I will drink it, and then—" The words are poison on my tongue, but I say it anyway. "I will desire you and only you for the rest of our lives. And our lives are bound to last thousands upon thousands of years."

"The love potion wouldn't be necessary if you pledged yourself to me through a blood oath. Old Iridion told me about blood oaths and their side effects before we left for the Seelie Realm—it would make us fated mates."

If my heart could freeze, it would. She must have asked old Iridion for ways to forge a mates' bond. She's determined to have my heart in her hands before the wedding.

"We could do it right now," she continues, undulating her body into mine. "What's to stop us from slashing our wrists with our fingernails, and drinking each other's blood?"

"Minerva." My whisper comes out cracked. She's trying to corner me, and she's succeeding, because indeed, this intimate moment would be perfect for a blood oath. Intimacy replaces the need for holy ground, and I have no real reason to refuse. There's only way out of this.

My hands slip down to her backside. I cup her butt cheeks, my fingers sinking into her white flesh. She gasps, gripping tightly to my shoulders, her want for me heightening. Her skin feels like butter on my fingertips, which makes my flesh crawl, my body chemistry rejecting her.

For Minerva, it's a different story. The chemistry of the Ice King appeals to all female fae, because of its promise to deliver special babies. She wants to rut like animals, and I have no choice but to play on that desire. I knead her butt cheeks, pushing my hips into her naked body. I conjure the sight of Arielle, and her scent in my mind, which is enough to trigger an erection. My cock becomes steel hard as I rub against Minerva with Arielle's face in my mind.

"Don't think I don't desire you," I say in a low, rumbling voice that makes Minerva moan, her eyes hooded. "What man wouldn't? I was just determined to focus on our task until the wedding, but I can't resist you, if you come on to me like this." Inside my head, I'm talking to Arielle. It's the only way I can express burning desire credibly.

I have no choice but to sleep with Minerva, but when I scoop her up and start towards the bed, she squirms.

"Put me down, I want to feel you in my mouth." But I can hear panic in her voice. The rush of desire is gone from her skin, and she's only trying to distract me with a blowjob. She glances at the bed, and then right back at me, but one instant was enough. I already spotted the dried demon eye tucked between the silken pillows.

We're not alone.

Arielle

MY JAW IS SO TIGHT that it hurts. On the inside, I'm about to combust.

The mates' bond was a side effect of the blood oath, an effect that Lysander didn't see coming, but he'll surely find a way to free himself of it when this is all over. When he doesn't need me anymore. Then, he intends to bind himself to Minerva.

Sure, she sent her servant to deliver me the dried demon eye and tell me when I should start watching, but she's not the one staging what's happening in Lysander's chamber. It's him who touches her greedily, and tells her he's only been playing me all this time.

I wish I could look away from the eye that has transformed into a scrying globe, not do this to myself, but I can't. I watch as Lysander drops Minerva on the bed in a rush of passion, but right that moment the doors to my chamber open, distracting me.

It's Zillard Dark.

"You sure know how to make an entrance, but this is getting old," I bark.

"I knocked. You didn't answer, but I knew you were inside. I worried something might have happened." He glances from me to the demon eye I'm holding, then stands aside.

"Let's go."

"I'm busy."

"We're not going to make any progress in your magic training if you take days off. Plus, you need to work what you just saw out of your system."

I hold out the demon eye. "So you have a hand in this?"

"Of course I do. How do you think Minerva had access to that kind of black magic, if not through a warlock?"

"If you help my rival, how do you expect me to ever trust you?"

"I only helped your rival in order to get through to you. I don't believe you can trust Lysander. Something's fishy about him."

"Oh, so you did this crap for me, not Minerva, is that right?"

"Right."

He sure can be cocky. But I've come to trust him. He was the only one who actually showed me how to use what I can access of my power, and taught me some magic, giving me the means to protect myself if I'm ever on my own.

And judging by what Lysander just told Minerva, I should expect to be on my own quite a lot.

I pocket the eye and follow Zillard into the castle gardens with my head high. This time I don't even try to hide, especially when we pass by Sandros, who's sitting on a high platform in a tree, polishing his blade. He stops working and stares at us like he can't believe it. In the end, Zillard and I have been keeping our meetings secret, and shrouded in shadow, so this must come as a shock. But I want Lysander to hear of me strolling around on Zillard's arm. I want to show him he doesn't have power over me, like he bragged to Minerva that he does.

I slip my arm around Zillard's, parading with him. The dark warlock flashes a smug grin at Sandros as he leads me further through the gardens.

The Seelie Fae realm is the most enchanted place I've ever seen, as if cut out of a very vivid fantasy dream. The Seelie are the most reclusive kind of fae, but also one of the oldest. They possess primordial knowledge that would be deadly in the hands of power-monger supernaturals such as Xerxes, so it makes sense that they're so secretive.

The Seelie King already declared he would remain neutral in the war between Lysander and Xerxes, if such an open war ever starts, but before that happens he offered the grounds for a neutral meeting with Calabriel Seawrath. I took part in some of Lysander's talks with him, even if only from the shadows, not sitting at the table of the mighty, where only Minerva had a place.

From the gardens, Zillard and I enter a deep forest of ancient trees with heavy crowns, fairy dust floating through the silky grass, the woods teeming with magic. The air here would be enough to cure humans of any disease, as well as mental and emotional trauma, but unfortunately it can't do anything to get my mind off of Lysander and Minerva. I see them in my head, rutting like beasts, and I can barely resist the searing temptation of using the demon eye to confirm my fears. My heart crumples as I imagine Lysander enjoying Minerva's fae body, licking her milky skin, then dipping his tongue inside her sweet-tasting pussy. Moaning between her folds, savoring her.

Bile rises to my throat.

"Zillard," I manage, trying to shake those tormenting scenarios from my head. "Is there any way, any magic that can help to lessen the emotional power someone has on you?"

"Get rid of romantic feelings, you mean?" He walks with his hands behind his back like an ancient wizard, somehow trapped in a young body. "Depends on the emotional attachment. If it's real and profound, there's no way to get rid of it permanently. You can lessen the effect, but think of all those couples who could never be together, but their feelings were so intense that they never really got over each other. They died thinking of one another."

I can imagine dying with Lysander's name on my lips. Cursing him and the day I laid eyes on his beautiful face.

Zillard and I emerge from the trees into scenery that takes my breath away. I gasp, slapping a hand on my chest.

"This is incredible," I breathe, staring at the huge silver moon hanging low in the sky, casting her silver light over the surface of a stunning cobalt blue lake.

Zillard stops in place, but I move forward, gravel crunching under my feet, fresh, pure air filling my lungs. Fairy dust sparkles over the crystalline shore where the water laps over the gravel. I need to feel all this wonder on my skin, sensing that it would replenish my tanks of vital energy.

I toe off my shoes and walk into the water, barefoot, feeling the gravel and the fresh water between my toes.

"God, this feels heavenly." It doesn't wipe the memory of Lysander and Minerva from my head, but it dampens it.

Then the water begins to sparkle. Zillard is hunkered down beside me, drawing a circle on the water circle, his index finger sending fine ripples through it. The ripples meet in the center, forming a kind of liquid mirror inside Zillard's circle. The sparkling came from his magic.

"Wicked," I breathe, fascinated, and crouch down by his side. I've seen enough of his quirks these past few days that they don't scare me anymore. If anything does, it's the fact that we might be becoming friends.

"It's a scrying mirror," he explains.

He's been training me for days, in secret. With my natural sea powers chained, and with Aunt Miriam's gift hiding deep in my powerhouse, becoming better at regular magic seems like my only option to gain some control over my own destiny.

"What are we looking at?" I scowl at the fine ripples. All I can make out is the outline of a city, or a town, until the landscape narrows down to a dark alleyway that reminds me of Gothic novels.

"At our secret weapon against Xerxes. If anything can bring him down, it's this. Look closer."

Lysander

I STOMP DOWN TO THE great hall, where we're finally meeting Calabriel Seawrath. My cape billows behind me, and my armor clatters, all in unison with my raging emotions. Warriors follow me with rigid faces. I feel feral, and that's the energy I give out. I'm thirsty for Zillard Dark's black blood.

Because of him, Arielle saw and heard my discussion with Minerva in the demon eye. The thought that she might have given herself to Zillard in order to punish me is tearing me apart. I have no doubt the bastard has taken advantage.

The grand doors open into a large hall with a domed ceiling that mirrors the skies, and water flowing down the opal walls, grand and splendid. The arched windows open to the impressive Seelie forests. Calabriel Seawrath is already waiting.

"King Lysander Nightfrost, Lord of the Winter Realm, King of Frost and rightful bearer of the Ice Crown," he states my full title, but bows his head only so slightly. He never liked me, and the feeling is mutual.

He's wearing a long glittery garment of greens, blues and gold, and his head, surprisingly, is bald. Which is what stops me in my tracks, and softens the expression on my face, replacing it with curiosity.

"Calabriel Seawrath, Steward of the Seas," I greet, approaching him. We stand face to face, holding each other's stare. He's smaller than me, and his baldhead makes the disparity even more striking. A thin, transparent layer of slime covers his skin, and his lips are bluish, livid. Sea fae and merfolk often come with smooth scales and sleek skin, yet the scales look and feel like jewels, and the skin is bright and healthy. I wonder if Calabriel is sick. His head looks like that of an octopus.

"I was just congratulating Lady Minerva on your recent engagement," he says with a grin that reveals widely-spaced teeth. I imagine the comment is enough to make this awkward for Minerva. They used to be lovers, something I'm not supposed to know. Now I understand why she left him—he looks nothing like what he used to. He changed so much these past few years.

"Please, sit," I invite, pointing to one of the intricately woven chairs with silken cushions. Servants hurry with carafes of nectars and juices, laying them right next to the rich bowls of fruit.

"We could cut right to the chase, King Lysander," Calabriel begins as his servants hold his robe, so he can take his seat comfortably. Minerva sits down by my side. She moves to place her hand over mine as I sit back in my seat, but then changes her mind. I must be emitting forbidding energy.

"So, to avoid unnecessary introductions, I know why you and Lady Minerva requested this extraordinary meeting. You want me as an ally in your conflict with Xerxes Blazeborn, which could explode into military action any day now." He waves his hand casually after one of his servants hands him a golden goblet of nectar. "To be frank, I didn't even want to come, if it weren't for one detail that intrigues me. By the way, where is our host, the Seelie King, won't he be joining us?"

"He's already made his choice, and he didn't want to influence you," I reply. I try to keep my tone even, but it's hard to hide how his nasal and arrogant voice gets on my nerves. "We're here to discuss yours."

"My choices are not up for discussions, thank you very much."

A corner of my mouth rises in a half-smile as I stare at him from under my eyebrows.

"Then why *did* you agree to meet me?"

He downs his nectar, then taps the goblet with his fingers, staring at me with a stroke of defiance.

"I would like to meet her." His small eyes glitter. "The ocean king's descendant. I understand you have proclaimed yourself her guardian, so I have to go through you. I believe the proper term would be 'legal guardian' in the mortal world, if you actually had any rights over her. Maybe I can remind her that you don't."

"Lysander found her," Minerva chimes in.

"This isn't a finders-keepers game, my sweet," he blocks. "If she really is the ocean king's rightful heir, then the King of Frost has no right to keep her prisoner."

"She cannot handle her own powers," Minerva explains. "She's been raised in the mortal world, is only twenty-two human years old, she is a baby with the button to launch a nuke at her fingertips."

"Still, it is not for you and the King of Frost to decide her fate."

"If Xerxes had found her in my place," I say, "you wouldn't be sitting here so well-served and cozy, Calabriel. He would have mated her, reinstated her in her rightful position, and would be using the oceans according to his whims. If that's the scenario you long to see, then by all means, sit back and just let the war come to pass. If he wins, you have a hundred percent chance of losing your position as Steward, and Xerxes taking over your reign. Should I tell you what will come of you, if this happens, or can you draw your own conclusion?"

He knows as well as I do that Xerxes would cut him into pieces, and spread his body throughout the ocean.

I can read Calabriel's inner struggle in his face as he watches me, chewing on the inside of his cheek.

"Becoming your ally could be trouble, too," he says. "Xerxes will have his allies, too, one can't know who one might upset in choosing your side. What if he has Tartarus on his side? Because I can't see Hades on yours."

"Hades isn't on our side, but he won't act against us either. His son, Zillard, is with us."

Calabriel's slick eyebrows rise. "The dark warlock? The half-demon?"

"I'd say he's a whole demon, but that's beside the point. He's taken a fancy to the heiress." I hiss the last word. "I gather they're together all the time lately."

"Zillard is my teacher," Arielle's crystalline voice fills the hall. "I learn magic from him—he's the only one willing to help me with that."

Both Calabriel and I stand as she approaches, the blood pounding wildly in my veins. The pale-blue gown glitters on her, the corset with a long, flowing skirt having become her signature. But in addition to that she's wearing a sapphire necklace that rests beautifully on the delicious swell of her breasts. Her shiny hair is up in a royal hairdo, and deep blue lace snake up her arms.

Her royal beauty knocks the air from my lungs. Never has a woman affected me like this. I want to pull her in my arms, and ravage her mouth with my kisses, marking her as mine, making it clear to the entire world that there will be blood if anyone tries to take her away from me. Controlling myself has never been harder.

Calabriel circles her, his eyes traveling all over her body. I want to punch him in the face for it, and Minerva is dying to slap me—I can feel her. I try to get a grip and rip my eyes away from Arielle, but the mates' bond is messing with my head big time.

"The woman who inherited the oceans," Calabriel whispers, inspecting her as if she were a circus curiosity. "Half-fae. Half human. A half-breed, inheriting the entire power of the waters. Incredible."

"A simple castellan having found his way to all that power is just as impressive, I assure you," Arielle strikes back. My chest swells with pride. Everything about her is gracefully aristocratic.

"I was just the next best thing after family, that's all." He grins.

"How lucky for you."

"If Zillard Dark isn't your lover," Calabriel changes the subject, "does that mean you're up for grabs?"

"Interesting choice of words. Ruffian even. I don't think I've ever heard a fae use it."

"Forgive me. I thought it would make you feel more at home, using human slang."

"How come you're familiar with the way mortals speak?"

"Scrying mirrors. I find humans fascinating." He motions to a chair. "Please, sit with us."

Minerva stiffens as Arielle approaches. I can smell her hatred for my mate, it stains the air around us with a sulfurous waft.

Calabriel holds a chair for Arielle, and servants hurry with the choice of carafes.

"I should like to hear as much as possible about your life among the humans," he says. "Not many of us have gotten the chance to experience it."

"My father lived in the human world for thousands of years. He must have told you a thing or two, I understand you were already a castellan at the time he returned to the Flipside." She doesn't even try to veil the implication that Calabriel might have had a hand in her father's assassination, but he chooses to ignore it.

"Your 'guardians' and I were just discussing my Court joining you on this quest of annihilating Xerxes' threat." He looks at me, once again avoiding an uncomfortable subject. "They made it clear that my Court is as much at stake as theirs. But that doesn't mean an alliance with you is my only option. I could, for example, strike a deal with Xerxes. He might yet have the more powerful allies. Rumor has it the Seelie King will remain neutral, while Xerxes might have already secured the darker Courts to aid him. There are things I can offer Xerxes, I'm sure we could reach an agreement."

Minerva opens her mouth to say something, but Arielle does it first.

"There are things that we can offer you, too, in exchange for your help."

"Oh yes?" he raises his eyebrows, moving his head theatrically her way. "Examples?"

"Let us play a game—it will ease some tension, and make the whole thing more pleasant, I should think." Arielle picks up her nectar goblet, and leans back gracefully, crossing her legs, looking like an ethereal queen.

"Let's pretend we are each other's genie, you and I. Tell me one wish that I and only I can make come true."

He grins, his eyes traveling down her body to make a point. "Just one wish?"

My blood rushes like an avalanche, and Minerva swallows uncomfortably. It must be unpleasant, watching your old boyfriend flirt openly with another woman, so I guess it makes two of us in this.

I can feel Arielle through our bond. She's disgusted, but manages to smile anyway.

"I'll start, if you like," she says.

Yes, the bastard likes that.

"I want the Trident."

He bursts into laughter. "No more and no less than the Trident, you say? Yes, sure, why would that even be a problem?" He laughs harder.

Arielle shrugs. "If you won't give us your support, then we'll be fine with the means to support ourselves. Zillard says the Trident commands the ocean beasts, both from the magical realms, and the human world. It wouldn't be you wielding it, so you wouldn't attract Xerxes' wrath. You can release the information that the Trident has been stolen, and—" She looks around. "Nobody is listening, right? This is a top secret meeting?"

"It's private, you can speak freely," Calabriel rushes her.

She gives him a smile that knocks him back. The presence of water infuses her with energy and beauty. Her cheeks have caught a peachy hue, and her blue eyes sparkle under her heavy black lashes. I can't help wanting to step in between her and Calabriel, and remind her that I'm the only man with the right to her seductive smiles.

"If you choose *not* to help us," she tells Calabriel, leaning closer to him as if telling him a secret, "I will claim the Sea Court when this is over. You can make a deal with Xerxes, but he will only fulfill it if he wins, or better yet, until he does. He might dispose of you afterwards anyway. If King Lysander wins, he will sustain my claim to the Sea Throne, and you won't have a chance to fight that claim. Isn't that so, Lord of Winter?" She meets my eyes.

"It is."

"Please don't think I don't understand, Lord Seawrath," she continues addressing him, while she holds my gaze. "I know you're faced with a very tough choice. Probably the toughest one ever. But while you weigh the pros and cons, please do not forget—Lord Lysander and I can be just as dangerous as Xerxes."

We keep staring at each other for moments, while Calabriel ponders.

"You said one wish," he eventually says. "There is one thing, actually, that you and only you can do for me. *Besides* the promise that you would not claim the Sea Throne when this is over."

She lifts her goblet at him with a wide, pearly smile. "I knew you'd see reason. But my promise not to claim the throne should suffice, don't you think? It means I'm giving up my entire legacy."

"Not your *entire* legacy—you retain your power over the seas. You see where I'm going? What's the point of ruling the seas if there's someone who can raise the waves against you, and wipe you out. So this, how shall I call it, *abdication* of yours isn't worth as much as you make it sound, and I have a hunch you know that. So here's my proposition—You promise not to claim the Sea Throne when this is over, and you'll fulfill one other wish for me. In return, I will join in this war with all of my forces, and I will secure you another new and powerful ally, too."

"What ally?" Minerva says. Her voice is harsh, as if they'd never been lovers.

Calabriel keeps silent for a heavy moment, creating tension. "Dragonblood shifters."

Dragonbloods. Serpent shifters, engineered into existence in the human world by shady corporations. The only supernaturals, besides Dracula's vampires and a few isolated werewolf clans, that are allowed to live in the human world, and that is only because they were 'born' there.

"Xerxes wants control over earth," Calabriel says, picking up his goblet and putting things into perspective. "The realm at the center of them all. Having allies there would up your chances of tipping everything in your favor."

Arielle looks at me questioningly, looking for guidance.

Dragonbloods are grim creatures, but they're powerful. Skilled assassins, swift, smooth. Their creators used snake DNA to make them, but they only used a particular kind of viper that's a direct descendant of dragons, which is why some of the engineered creatures can actually shift into dragons. It is increasingly difficult for them to keep their nature secret in the human world, though, becoming so large when they shift. Calabriel must have given them shelter on the Flipside during their phases, which is why he has access to them.

Through our mates' bond, my thoughts are enough for Arielle to understand. Still, she acts too quickly-

"All right, I agree to your terms," she declares. "Now what wish shall I fulfill for you?"

"You promise to do it, no matter what I request?"

"No, she doesn't," I flare. "Let us hear it, and then she'll decide."

He addresses Arielle. "I want you to retrieve the Pearl of Riches for me."

Arielle frowns. "The Pearl of Riches. Is that what I think it is?"

I burst into laughter.

"I'm glad you find this amusing, King of Frost," Calabriel says, offended.

"No, it's just—" I clear my voice. "Now I understand what happened to your hair." And the rest of his beauty.

Greed caused him to lose it. For the fae, the outer body is an expression of the inner energy. Ignoble feelings cause fae to lose certain parts of their beauty. Minerva, for example, lost the celestial sweetness of her face because of a meanness not suitable for us. The strict lines of a harsh dame replaced that sweetness. Of course, she's far from ugly, and some men would actually prefer her like this, but her face is special for a fae.

But things are different for Calabriel, because there's no sexy side to greed. And it's probably not the only thing that's plaguing him.

"Let me tell you something, King of Frost," Calabriel says pointedly. "It's easy to despise those who love riches when you own outrageous amounts of them, beside a High Fae title. Like your princess here said, I am only a castellan, only a steward of the seas, and will never be more than that. Class is a petrified thing in our world, even though we're so much older and think ourselves much more advanced than the humans. The only way I can secure myself the favors of a woman of standing, is to become rich beyond imagination."

His eyes slip over to Minerva. I can see that everything between them is over, and I don't think Calabriel actually wants her back, but it's clear he wants to marry his way to a title. She must have hurt him deeply. Maybe the negative emotions that he experienced when she left were what destroyed his outer fae beauty. He sure looks at her like she's the person who took everything away from him. I know Minerva well enough, she's capable of that and more.

"I'll do it," Arielle interrupts my stream of thought. My eyes become slits.

Cunning fills Calabriel's face, giving substance to my worries. "Fabulous."

"Do I have to search for it, or do you know where it is, and just have trouble retrieving it?"

"Oh, I do know where it is. The Sea Witch has it."

That's it. I spring off the chair, my hand flashing around the bastard's neck. I lift him from the ground, his face swelling violet within seconds.

"Did you actually think this cheap trick would work? Asking the impossible of her?"

"It's not the impossible, Lysander, and you know it," Minerva intervenes, standing. "If anyone can get to the Sea Witch, it's her. This is really a wish that only Arielle de Saelaria can fulfill." Her sharp blue eyes throw blades at me. I think she's beginning to see through my pretenses. She's beginning to understand that I'm truly into Arielle, and not just playing on her feelings.

"Lord Lysander, please," Arielle's crystalline voice reaches me. "Put him down, let him talk. See if he can explain."

I hesitate, but then set Calabriel down on his feet. I'd like a fucking explanation, too. He buckles over with a hand at his throat, coughing, feeling for his chair. He drops into it, downing Arielle's goblet of nectar.

"The Sea Witch," he manages, his voice still hoarse. "No one has seen her in centuries. She went into hiding because my Court is hunting her down for having massacred the royal family. But you." He looks at Arielle. "Killing you is still her greatest ambition, because she blames her situation today on your father having escaped her grand massacre in his mother's belly thousands of years ago. So she's probably dreamed up ways to torture you before she kills you. If go near water and think of her intensely, she'll surely hear you. You're actually the only person in the world she'd show herself to."

And Arielle wants to see her, because Zillard got her thinking she could lift the silver spell.

"I will lift it," I tell her, my eyes burning. "I'll lift the silver spell, you don't have to go to her, she'll kill you."

"Lysander," Minerva shrieks. "What are you doing?"

Being desperate. Right now I wouldn't care if the world went down in flames. All I care about is preventing Arielle from going on a suicide mission.

"Lysander," Minerva insists when I don't break eye contact with my mate. "If you lift the spell, her powers will overwhelm her. She hasn't had enough training. It would probably make it even easier for the Sea Witch to kill her."

"I'll go with you," I tell Arielle.

"No," Calabriel protests. "The Sea Witch will never reveal herself if Arielle isn't alone. The risk of assassination is too great."

"But what makes you think she'll give me the Pearl of Riches," Arielle inquires. "She wants me dead, I doubt she'll sit down to do business with me first."

"She doesn't want to just kill you. Like I said, she'll want to make you suffer first, which will give you time to search."

"You're not taking this into consideration, no!" I snarl, but Arielle ignores me.

"How will I search for anything if she keeps me in chains?"

Calabriel massages his neck, where my grip has left a red mark. "Your not-boyfriend Zillard Dark will have the answer to that."

"This is madness, none of this is happening," I rumble.

"Suit yourself, Lysander," Calabriel says. "But think about it—the Pearl of Riches and your protégé's abdication is what I require to grant you my full support against Xerxes, and to bring in hordes of experienced, engineered fighters. Think of everything I'm putting on the table."

Minerva's cold, slippery hand slides into mine. "Yes, Lysander." Threat shadows her voice, a threat that's directed at Arielle. "Think of everything that's at stake."

CHAPTER V

Arielle

"What did it feel like?" Zillard asks as we sit face to face by the lake, my hands in his, palms facing upwards. "Having Lysander so close again?"

Small bluish circles spin in the middle of my palms, enabling me to call forth a liquid portal between realms, using the lake. It's supposed to work with any kind of water, anywhere, and save me from the Sea Witch once the mission is complete.

"It..." I see Lysander's strong warrior features in my mind, his intense blue stare that made me feel like the only woman in the world. I remember creaming between my legs from the intensity alone. I felt desired to the point of madness, which made me ache to fall to my knees and take his cock into my mouth.

"He tried to play me again, acting every bit the passionate lover."

"But you didn't fall for it?"

"After I've seen him almost fuck Minerva with my own eyes, after I heard from his own mouth how he only pretended to be impassionate for me in order to manipulate me? I'd be a complete idiot to fall for any of his acting ever again. But he's pretty damn good at it, I'll give him that. I remember the day we met. He was the perfect ice king, empty of all emotions. I can't believe he is able to pretend so well."

Zillard lowers his head, as if about to share a long kept secret.

"What is it?"

"Listen, Arielle." He takes a deep breath, making a hard decision. "Before you go on your quest, there's something I need to tell you. When I first met Minerva—she came to my chamber back at Lysander's castle, the night before the engagement ball—she told me Lysander despised you, but that you were planning to use your love spells on him on the big day. She asked me to counter your spells with my magic. That is the true reason why I approached you at the ball—If I was close enough, I could block your magic before it left your personal field. But when I saw the way Lysander looked at you... I had a strong impression his feelings for you were real. Later, when Minerva asked me for the demon eye, it raised further doubts."

"What doubts?"

"She said that, spells or no, you were using your lowly water nymph magic to separate them, and somehow it was working. But then I watched him more closely. I know he sent people to follow you ever since we came here, and he was growing crazier by the day, thinking you and I were having an affair."

He stops talking, and looks deep into my eyes out of his demonic irises.

"Have you ever wondered why I'm helping you, Arielle? Why I teach you magic, protect you?"

"Yes. But I was afraid to ask."

"Afraid, because you expected that I was in love with you?"

"Not, not in love. But interested."

"Then let me tell you the truth now."

"I'm not sure I want to know."

"Yes, you do. You won't like it any more than the first version though, the one in which I was in love with you."

I frown, waiting for it. My throat closes up.

"Minerva approached me before the engagement day, taking advantage of the fact that it had been Sandros who invited me, and whatever happened to you, it couldn't be traced back to her. She paid me to get close to you, block your magic if you used it and, of course, seduce you, if I found you to my liking."

"You wouldn't have stood a chance at seducing me, Zillard." Even though he is irresistibly handsome, darkly so. But I'm cursed to want only Lysander for the rest of my life, crave him to the point of insanity.

"Yes, well, I would have found ways to make you want me. Arielle, I'm more than just the son of Hades. My mother was a demoness, a succubus. Seducing people is in my nature. I feed on their life energy, on their souls. Now, no offense but, for reasons that I didn't understand at the time, you didn't appeal to me, you know, *that* way. But the second time I came into your life didn't have to do with Minerva, or anyone else. What called to me was the dark power that your aunt Miriam willed to you."

"How do you know that Aunt Miriam willed me anything?"

He takes a deep breath. "Because my father, Hades, foresaw it. In your case, he only had the premonition a few minutes before it happened. When Lysander made the decision to ask for Miriam's help."

"Why would the god of Tartarus foresee what would happen with me or Aunt Miriam?"

"Arielle, Hades, my father—" He licks his lips. "He is also your Aunt Miriam's father."

I swear the world has just stopped. I can feel my jaw drop in slow motion.

"What the hell are you telling me?"

"In a way, we're family, Arielle. I am your uncle, I guess, even if not by blood. When Miriam ceded you her dark powers, you and I, we became related. More or less like siblings. And now my father Hades has a personal stake in this. He needs Lysander to win and make you Queen of the sea Court."

I get up to my feet. "You mean to fucking tell me that I have a piece of Hades inside of me?"

"You needed to know all of this before you exposed yourself to the Sea Witch. If push comes to shove, trust me—use Miriam's power."

I shake my head, looking up at the moon, its light mirrored in the dark ripples of the lake.

"The Sea Witch," I whisper, wondering where she could be hiding, and how many ways of torturing me she must have imagined all these years. I wonder when she'll find me, and how, and whether or not I'll be ready for it.

I'm scared, but I know that the sooner she finds me, the better. We don't know how long we have until Xerxes pulls out the big guns.

I put up my palms, and conjure the water swirls in their center. The Sea Witch is bound to sense a water portal that's connected to me, if I'm thinking of her. I'm not ready, but as ready as I'll ever be. It's now or never.

"Do you want me to be here when you return?" I hear Zillard's deep dark voice behind me.

I ponder. Do I want to see him again, the guy who planned to seduce my soul out of me before he realized I was some kind of a sister to him? But as I focus on the portal, I'm all feeling and no mind. And in that feeling there's no space for grudges.

"Family is family, right?" I whisper, my voice already spectral. I'm being pulled into my magic, my mind shutting down. With it, so does fear.

The surface of the lake starts to rotate, rising like the base of a tornado. In a few seconds, I feel its force pull on the small swirls in my palms like a magnet. The wind increases, blowing through my hair, and I can sense it when Zillard steps back.

"It's time," he says.

I close my eyes, giving in to the feeling of magic, letting it take over my body and chase away the all too human feeling of anxiety. I step into the water, walking slowly towards the swirl. It sucks me in, its force like that of a centrifuge tugging at my flesh to tear me apart.

It spits me out into a roasting heat that smacks me right in the crown of my head. I look up, shading my eyes from the brightest sun that has ever touched my skin. In a few seconds my eyes adjust and I make out the landscape. If this is the Sea Witch's prison, she must have thought long and hard about it, because there's no way I could have foreseen it.

It's a desert. As far as I can see, there's only dunes of sand, with the sun as the only guidance. I start walking towards the East, my naked feet sinking into the hot sand, with nothing to dampen the burn. I walk on my tiptoes and the sides of my feet, my mouth dry af.

I don't know how long it's been when the sun finally begins its descent into the bloody horizon, but I know that my lungs are burning, and I could kill for a little bit of water. I'd gladly give in to a mirage and trick myself into believing I'm having a drink.

The sun goes down completely, and I drop onto the sand, exhausted. The temperature drops quickly, too quickly. Soon it's so cold that I curl up into a fetal position, hugging myself and wishing I'd freeze to death, and be spared this torture. Wind whips sand through my hair and over my face. My flesh cracking open, and sand sticks to my wounds. I curse myself for not having thought of this—How can I ever get what I came for, if the Sea Witch won't even let me see her, or talk to me. I should have expected the possibility that she wouldn't interact with me at all, that she'd go directly to killing me slowly. Was I naive to think that she'd want me to see her before I die, that she'd want her voice to be the last thing I hear?

In the dead of night, maddened with thirst, I lick at the cold sand, hoping to find a layer of frost. Why do I cling to life like this, when I know for a fact that I'm going to die?

"Playing with portals, little princess?" a throaty voice slips into my mind. *"Didn't your auntie warn you about the dark things that lurk in the unknown realms?"*

I raise my head a few inches, which is all I can. *"You're the reason I opened that portal, Sea Witch, and you know it."*

"Please, call me Ursula. If you've been looking for me as I have for you, then we're almost soulmates, don't you think?" She giggles, but it's a nasty sound.

"Please, I'm desperate for water. And for your help. I will offer you anything in return."

"Anything?"

"My rightful claim to the sea throne. I'll cede it to you, if you lift the silver spell that Lysander Nightfrost has put over my sea powers. That's why I went out looking for you."

"You cannot give me the throne, girl, because it's not yours to give. The Steward glued his greedy ass to it, and he's never vacating it again—trust me, I have tried to get rid of him every way possible. Besides, I've had that throne before. I didn't hold it for long. The merfolk have found a way to banish me, and they will again, no matter how often I claw my way to power. My only goal now is to make them all suffer."

Fuck.

"There must be something I can give you," I reply, desperately sifting through my mind for something. *"I am the ocean king's heiress after all."*

"Of course there's something—your life. But not abruptly. No, I've been dreaming of ways to end Poseidon's bloodline for so long, I'm going to savor

every moment of your slow, painful passing. I will take my time with you, Arielle de Saelaria, and have you die a hundred deaths. The spirit of your grandfather will see it and live it all with you from the highest realm where he now dwells, he will suffer with you. He'll be aware the whole time that this is happening because he chose that water nymph over me. It was never a problem that he had lovers, I had lovers, too, but if he was ever to share the throne, he was supposed to share it with me!"

I can't believe it, is this what the massacre of the Sea Court was about? Was the Sea Witch a scorned woman?

Her voice is fading. She's leaving me here.

"Please, don't go," I cry, but her presence is fading in the distance.

Exhausted and desperate, I drop my head into the sand. A curled, crusty little tail emerges from the ground, quivering its way closer. I don't dare move. I know it's a scorpion before the animal's body appears from behind the little dune. And I know there's nothing I can do to stop it from stinging me.

I can't move my battered body abused by the elements. My clothes are rags that flap wildly, hitting my skin like whips. I can feel sand creep into the cracks on my lips as the beast moves closer, its tail touching my hand as if sniffing it.

God, what I wouldn't do for a little bit of water right now. Not to drink it, but to use it to try and conjure a portal. But the Sea Witch thought of that, of course. As a daughter of the ocean, I would find salvation in water. I sift through the magic that Zillard has taught me, feverishly looking for something to help me.

He taught me the fetching spell, and magnetizing my hands to receive the object—for when I find the Pearl of Riches. He helped me amplify my telepathic abilities, and channel healing energy to my palms, which went smoothly. Telepathy is an innate talent of mine, he said, and with healing I have some experience. But I could do it a lot better if I had full command over my sea powers.

Scrying is the last magic that would bring something of use into this situation, and the glamour tricks won't be of much use either, but...It hits me.

I close my eyes and think of Zillard. I run my hand once over my face, without touching it, and create a glamour.

If the Sea Witch is watching me now it's not the dried out shell of a woman in the desert that she sees, but the seductive Zillard Dark, son of Hades. Sooner or later, she will have to check in again.

When she does, the sun is rising. I raise my face to it, letting the first rays warm me up. That's when I feel her watching me. She would be confused, of course, but only for a few moments. The confusion won't last long, so I use the little strength I still have, and do what I do best. I murmur a love spell that needs only small amounts of water. I call on what's left of the water in my own system. It won't be very powerful, for that I'd need the Sea Witch here, so I can bind the spell to her blood, but it will do to pique her interest.

But I'm afraid the spell is too weak, because there's too little water in my body. If I use any more,

The sun darkens, transforming into a black hole within a ring of fire, a black hole that approaches. It opens up to swallow me, blowing the hair from my face, my rags flapping around my body. I open my arms and let it take me.

The portal sucks me in and drops me on all fours on what looks like clay. Humid air attacks the dryness in my throat, making me cough. When I get more or less a clear head, I realize that my hands don't look the way they did earlier in the desert. There, they were pruned, dehydrated to the point where I must have looked like a monster. Here, they look normal.

"You're powerful," I hear the witch's raking voice. I raise my eyes to a corpulent woman in a black corset that showcases voluptuous breasts, her skirt black, and strangely frayed at the rim. When the frays start to move, I shriek back. The woman grins, revealing white, razor-sharp teeth behind painted red lips. This isn't a woman, this is a beast.

"You used a glamour, and a love spell on me. A love spell that worked. Never has a love spell worked on or for me before, and trust me, I even commissioned quite a few—the last one for your grandfather, of course." She looks at me out of bulging eyes with super small irises, her hair like a wild white broom.

"I had to get your attention somehow." Using my throat comes surprisingly easy. I take my hand to it, touching smooth skin. "The desert. It was only an illusion?"

"What better prison than one's very own mind, if the illusion is masterfully created." She walks on the tentacles that form her black dress, and sits down on a cushioned stool in front of a make-up table. Behind it, a big studio mirror flashes the spotlights lining its frame, and I can see her better. My stomach turns. Her skin is a greyish-white, like a corpse, and the smell of rotten fish wafts over. She waves her hand at the mirror.

"Through this, I can see into my prisoner's mind. And I've seen a lot of minds, but none of them ever captivated me the way you did now." She gives me her abnormally large grin that makes the hair stand up on the back of my neck. "Clever of you to use that half-incubus hunk, Zillard Dark. Delicious young warlock. If only he weren't a soul eater."

Her scary eyes bulge at me.

"Fascinating inventions, the mirrors. If you'd had more time with Zillard, I'm sure he would have taught you this trick, too. But I forget. It's not that incubus you love. It is the King of Ice, the handsome warrior, Lysander Nightfrost."

My heart twists. "I don't *love* Lysander. Lysander robbed me of my powers. He is the reason I was looking for you. Zillard says you're the only one who can lift the silver spell."

"I *can* lift the spell."

"Will you do it?" I stare into her face like I actually mean it. I think part of me truly does.

"Tell me something little princess," she says, full of contempt. "Do you think I'm a complete idiot, to give the only living descendant of Poseidon complete power over the seas?"

A bitter taste forms in my mouth. "Maybe the throne isn't mine to cede, as you say, but with my power, I could support your claim to it."

"In that case all fae lords would unite to shut you down. Your support isn't worth much."

Okay, this isn't going how I planned. I look around, starting to think of ways to escape, with or without the Pearl of Riches. We're inside a cave with ribbons hanging down from the ceiling, a bed with fluffy pillows in a far alcove, and many colorful bottles and vials on rock shelves carved into the walls. Behind the Sea Witch, in the darker length of the cave, there's a table that seems made of clay, heavy with magical items.

"I need some water," I manage, my throat tight with panic. I can feel my control slipping.

The Sea Witch snaps her fingers, and a sparkling carafe floats in from the back. She sends it towards me, using magic that I've been practicing with Zillard, too. I grab the carafe with both hands and drink greedily. The rivulets escaping the corners of my mouth seem like a terrible waste.

I drink my fill and wipe my mouth on my sleeve. The Sea Witch watches me with keen interest, as if she's never seen a creature quite as interesting before.

"They say you're half human."

"I am."

"Fascinating." She turns to the mirror and picks a lipstick. "The power to command all seas flows through your veins, even though you're only fifty percent magical creature. I would have expected your human blood to dilute that power. Like magic is diluted in all hybrids. Well, in those not produced by fated mates."

"What do you mean, 'not produced by fated mates'?" I have to keep the Sea Witch talking while I activate my senses to track the Pearl of Riches, and then get out of here ASAP. I can feel the sea really close, its salty scent tantalizing my senses, so I should be able to create a portal once I have it.

"Haven't you heard?" she says. "Winter and sea fae tried re-creating the primordial Court of Ice and Sea by mating with each other, in order to produce hybrids with power over both elements. But to do that, they had to ignore the call of their natural mates. Problem is, it's those natural mating bonds that produce the best possible offspring. What the forced sexual alliances brought was, well, like I said, hybrids with dual, but diluted powers."

I just have to ask her. "Does that work with chosen mates, too? For High Fae, who can select their mates, I mean? Do those unions produce powerful offspring?"

"High Fae rarely choose mates that they don't fancy in the first place. If they fancy them, they're good matches."

"The one I'm asking about might have chosen someone he didn't like. It was an accident."

"Now you've piqued my interest." She comes over on her tentacles, and God, it looks eerie. "If you tell me who you're talking about, I might let you live longer."

"My father, and my human mother. He..." I decide to replace their story with my own. "He made a blood oath to her after she aided him in a fight, unaware that it would make them bonded mates as well."

"If that's the case, then you're indeed the best possible case study." She takes my hand, regarding it like a priceless artifact in a museum. She traces the fine, almost unnoticeable silver drawings under my skin with her finger. They light up under her touch, only to fade again when she moves along. "Set free, you would wield the entire ocean power, so that power wasn't diluted. Your other magic, that's not bad either. You're half human and half fae but I think with training, you'd make a pretty good black witch, too."

She sounds almost impressed, but I shudder. Black magic scares me. I only learned some from Zillard because I didn't have a choice, not really. It was my only means to protect myself.

"Little princess," the Sea Witch says darkly as she takes distance from me, floating into the shadows, where only the large whites of her eyes remain. "If you only knew how that love spell saved you. Maybe it can even buy your freedom—if you give me Zillard Dark."

The Sea Witch and Zillard? "You... you want his love?"

She laughs, the sound raising the finest hairs on my nape. "Love? I'm thousands of years old, little princess, I don't believe in worthless illusions such as love."

"That's what I thought," I mumble through my teeth, trying to push the image of my sort-of-brother Zillard in bed with this octopus.

"A night of lust will suffice," she says, zapping me with it. "Maybe two. But in those hours I want to feel all the might of his dark, twisted lust."

No!

"I can't give Zillard to you. What I did, it was nothing more than a hat trick, something to get you to pull me out of the desert."

"You'll do it," she snarls. "You will give him to me, you will put a spell of lust on him, or you'll join the rest of your family." The echoes of her croaking voice fill the cave, sending the sensation of cockroaches crawling all over my skin. Her eyes glow like a killer's in the dark, and her voice sounds of hell. "Maybe we should visit them. I'm sure you'll take it as an incentive."

"V-visit them?" I babble. Crippling fear creeps under my skin. But no, I won't let it take over me.

Tentacles slip under my armpits and coil around my shoulders, pulling me up. It's the Sea Witch's black octopus-dress that she can apparently lengthen as much as she likes. She moves father into the darkness, her tentacles pulling me after her, my toes raking the sand.

It's cold deeper in the cave, a damp chill that seeps into my flesh. I can hear water dripping, so we must be heading toward the sea. The smell of salt and seaweed grows stronger, feeding me vital energy. I feel stronger, even my muscles harden, the sea pumping strength back into them. But it won't be enough to defeat the ancient Sea Witch. Water is her natural environment, too, not to mention that her powers are at her best, and she's been around for thousands of freaking years. While I'm chained under Lysander's silver spell.

The tunnel turns sharply downwards. It feels like sliding down a gutter, until we reach an insulated underwater cave. I can feel the call of the sea all around it.

"There," the Sea Witch says, moving in the shadows to the side. Her tentacles slither off of me, putting me down on my own feet.

It's dark, but light reflects off a pond of water at the bottom of the cave, which seems pretty far down. The only sound disrupting the silence is the lapping, echoing against the wet stone walls. A cry rips through it, like that of an animal being stabbed. My back stiffens, and I walk closer to the edge of the platform where I'm standing, looking down.

Fog curls around the pond edges, but I think I see something moving through it. Then something else. Under any other circumstances I would shriek and jump back, which is probably the sane thing to do, but this feels different. Like the moving things are calling to me. I walk dangerously close to the edge. All the Sea Witch would have to do is give me a little push, and I'd fall into the foggy pond at the bottom.

I distinguish small, deformed bodies that look like shrunken, rat-like animals. A set of beady yellow eyes latch onto mine, and the creature releases a gut-wrenching cry. The fog slowly dissipates, revealing en entire horde of deformed beings that cry out at me, forming an unbearable echo, like they're being massacred.

I cover my ears and force myself to step back onto the safety of the platform, fighting the pull they have on me. They almost make me want to jump. The feeling of belonging to these creatures is overwhelming.

"*They are what's left of the people massacred at the ocean king's great ball,*" the Sea Witch speaks in my head, satisfaction behind her words. God, how I hate her. "*The ocean king's children by his numerous lovers. They are all here now because of your father, you know. The ocean king's almost-legitimate son. If Poseidon hadn't hidden him from me, if he hadn't done the impossible to save him, they would probably still be alive today. Well, not that they're not alive now, but they're pretty miserable, as you can see.*"

"*You devil. You wouldn't have spared them anyway.*"

"*Now, now, you don't have to believe everything they say about me. Why would I still want to annihilate these poor creatures, if I'd had the only one that mattered? I only needed to sacrifice the legitimate heir. You see, that old bastard never married any of his lovers, never intended to, and that meant none of his children had a legitimate claim to the sea throne. Until he met your grandmother. Oh, she had an almost magic hold on him. I suspect that's why you're so good with love spells—you inherited her talent.*"

I can feel her rolling around me on her tentacles, but I won't look at her. I can't lower my hands from my ears until I know the creatures have stopped whining and shrieking, I wouldn't be able to endure any more of that.

"Now, if your grandmother could enchant Poseidon himself to ask for her hand in marriage, then you should have no problem breathing carnal desire for me into Zillard Dark's blood. You do tie your spells to the males' blood, don't you? That's the technique you use?"

"It's the most effective one," I hiss telepathically.

"But that is a form of black magic, you know that, right?"

"Aunt Miriam didn't teach me magic in terms of black and white. Her books..." But I stop. It hits me—In secret, Aunt Miriam was a creature of darkness. Her father was Hades himself. That's probably why she rarely ever taught me any magic. At most she told me things, never showed me. I learned most of what I know from her books, many of which she kept under lock and key. I practiced on my own.

"Say the spell, Arielle." Now that we're far enough from the edge of the platform, the creatures have stopped shrieking, and the Sea Witch is using her voice again.

"I would need to be around him. Or, at the very least, I need something of his, so I can hook into his biology."

"Hmm." She ponders, circling me like a hideous black octopus with a human upper body. "Would a hair or a fingernail do?" She gives me that skin-crawling, razor grin of hers, but I repress the shudder. I won't show her any more fear, because the freaking banshee seems to be feeding on it.

"You're the bigger witch," I grunt. "You should know."

Her tentacles coil around my arms again, and pull me back towards the main cave. She lifts her hands in the air, her fingers wriggling, and an iron cage takes form.

Fuck. Iron is deadly to the fae.

"That should hold you." She tosses me inside, then slams the locks shut. "I wouldn't try to escape if I were you. Touching iron causes deadly rashes to the fae, from what I've seen." She grins, which speaks volumes about what she's done to other fae. "The fae's weakness to iron has baffled wizards and others keepers of knowledge for millennia, because it doesn't really make scientific sense. There's iron in your blood. But I can tell you where that weakness comes from, if you're curious." She stares at me through the bars out of her scary irises. "You're sensitive to iron because your flesh is made of a combination of nature's basic elements, namely air, ice, fire, water and earth—much less earth than human bodies. The elements harm and weaken iron. But, in the composition of your flesh, iron harms them back in the same way."

She retreats into the darkness, the long black tentacles trailing like an eerie bridal gown.

"I'll pay a short visit to your friend, Zillard Dark. Nothing to worry about, I'll send a sleeping spell ahead of me, so he doesn't get scared. If by some miracle you manage to escape the iron cage, beware. Your sweet family of sea goblins will start a concert that will drive you to kill yourself. So be a good girl, and wait for me quietly."

But there's one thing she doesn't take into consideration, and that I can use to advantage. I wait until I'm certain that she's gone, assessing my surroundings. I close my eyes, sampling the energetic vibration of the magic around, searching for other invisible weapons besides what's left of the original Sea Court.

Her black magic feels like cockroaches crawling over my skin.

Every item in this place has a dark vibe, and most of those vials are locked with protection spells strong enough to blow up the hand of anybody who tries to touch them. I seek the vibration of the Pearl of Riches, stilling my mind, and calming down my body. If anyone could see me now, I'd probably resemble a yogi monk whose spirit travels to other realms.

But I'm very much in my skin, feeling grateful for being only half fae, and for the fact that the Sea Witch didn't take that into consideration when she tossed me inside an iron cage. If my magic had been purely fae, I wouldn't be able to use much of it right now.

Surprisingly, I find it easy and even pleasant to put the darker side of me to use, tapping into the inky ripples of my powerhouse. My dark magic blends in well with the Sea Witch's signature, which makes the discovery of the Pearl of Riches beneath her pillows go unexpectedly smoothly. It's sort of like putting myself in her shoes—where would I keep it if I were her? Judging by her crib she's in love with luxury and riches, so she would keep it as close as possible. The moment I spot it my eyes snap open, and a satisfied smile forms on my face.

I stretch out my arm, palm open, murmuring the fetching spell and magnetizing the stone to me. Luckily, it doesn't have a protection spell on it, probably because the Sea Witch never expected anyone to reach it, since she sleeps with it under her pillow. Besides, it doesn't look particularly flashy. A small shabby shell travels through the air, slipping sideways between the bars, and landing in my hand. When I open it, it reveals a bright pearl, glowing like ivory. I'm proud of myself.

Time to get out of here. Tucking the shell in my panties, I start to design a plan in my mind. Even if I could conjure a water portal to transport me back to the lake, I can't use it because I'm caged, and this iron box is so small that the portal surely won't appear *inside*.

I close my eyes and feel into my powerhouse of magic, sifting through what I can do. Feeling out objects, magnetizing them, telepathy, love spells, glamour, and now I've picked up some of the Sea Witch's skill of peering into minds through a mirror. But none of that is going to help me. Unless...

I put out my palms, and activate the magnetic power I used with the fetching spell, trying to bend the bars. But apparently the magnetism only matches my own physical strength, which isn't nearly enough to bend the iron. I try harder, clenching my teeth, my lip curling over them. I salivate from the effort, but nothing happens.

Exhausted and breathing hard, I magnetize two hairpins from the vanity table, and try to pick the lock with them, but the one time I googled how it's done doesn't help much. I cry out in frustration.

Come on, Arielle, think.

I'm no longer the powerless girl who got thrown into Lysander Nightfrost's dungeon, now I'm a powerful fae, with the ability to control black magic. I have to be able to free myself.

I close my eyes, and turn to my last resort.

CHAPTER VI

Arielle

Sweat trickles down my forehead as I reach the one person I have a direct telepathic line to—Lysander.

"*I need help.*"

But all I get back is clamor, the sound of battle. My pulse accelerates.

"*What's happening, where are you?*"

A blade strikes into his armor, making me wince. My body is in an iron cage in the Sea Witch's lair, but my mind is firmly anchored in Lysander's.

I focus harder, trying to see through his eyes.

"*Don't,*" he blocks me just before another blade lands somewhere on his metallic body. "*I'll lose focus if you take over my eyes.*"

"*Where are you, what's going on?*" I insist.

"*Hang in there, Arielle. I'm coming for you.*"

His last words have a soft, longing sound to them. My knees melt, but then roaring blasts through my mind, ripping the connection and leaving me with a terrible ringing in my ears. I crouch to the floor, hands to my temples, pressing against the pain. The iron door opens, and when I raise my head, the Sea Witch stands in front of me. She holds out a black shirt that I recognize as Zillard's.

"Do it," she commands.

"I'm going to need some kind of guarantee that you won't kill or torture me after that," I manage, my temples still throbbing from the telepathic experience with Lysander. I'm going mad with worry about him.

She bares her razor teeth.

"If you pull this off, I'm going to ask it of you again. And again. For that, I'm going to need you alive, and maybe even comfortable."

"You want to make Zillard your sex slave?"

"And you're gonna be watching."

She drags me out of the cage, her stench of putrid fish making me gag. Only now I realize it's the stench of stale black magic. She tosses me by a black cauldron of seawater.

This is my last chance. I have to hi-jack this properly, otherwise I'm dead.

She throws his shirt in my face.

"There's a stain of blood on the collar. I put him to sleep and pricked him. You have the blood, so no excuses."

I glance from the cauldron of water to the shirt in my hands, but I can't even consider doing it. I close my eyes tightly, and hold out my palms, Zillard's shirt draped over them so the Sea Witch doesn't notice the blue swirls forming in my palms. I chant the spell in my head, conjuring seawater from the bowl to form a portal, putting all my energy into it so that it goes fast.

But it doesn't go fast enough. Realizing what I'm doing, the Sea Witch grunts, and slaps me hard with the back of her fleshy hand. The impact sends me tumbling over the cauldron. I push myself up from the floor, my hair and my rags drenched.

Something slices into the back of my thigh, white pain shooting through it. I scream, and look at my leg. There's a deep gashing wound, an iron hooked into it. My skin already starts to blacken around the metal.

"Jesus Christ," I cry.

"I guess it's going to be torture after all," the witch hisses, rising her big arms above me. Her hands grow like shadows, and her fingernails elongate, transforming into iron claws. My eyes widen in terror as she brings them down on me, and slices through my other leg.

I scream, and turn on my stomach, crawling away from her on my elbows, regretting the day I was born. I hear her tentacles rustling close behind, following me. She laughs, watching me crawl in agony away from her, leaving traces of blood behind. Jesus Christ, please let this be only a nightmare.

But no. She strikes again, this time my back. Her iron claws slash my rags and slice my loins. I cry out and thrash, which causes the Pearl of Riches to slip from its hideout. The Sea Witch lifts it up in one of her tentacles, inspecting it closely.

"You tried to steal the Pearl from me?" she snarls. "Is this why you were really here?"

"You don't understand," I manage through shallow breaths. "I-I need it to stop a war. It's not like I could have just asked for it."

"And if I'd helped you with your sea powers, those would have been a nice bonus, right?"

"If you'd agreed to help me, I would have been completely honest with you."

She shrieks and strikes again, full of hatred, but she misses me by an inch.

I creep into a corner, watching her grow larger, her big arms above her head. Her claws are stained with rust ready to do as much damage as possible.

Except, even though my wounds have started to blacken, I don't have quite the same aversion to iron as full fae. My wounds can be healed. I close my hands over the hook in my leg, focusing the healing energy into the wound. A few seconds, and I can already feel my flesh pushing out the hook.

I grimace at the devilish witch, making her think I'm going mad with pain. That way she won't hurt me again, she'll just enjoy the show. She takes delight watching me, unaware that I'm healing myself behind her back. And thinking of ways to annihilate her.

I've never felt pure hatred before in my life, but I'm pretty sure this is it. I look deep into her evil eyes as she raises those thin, arched eyebrows, realizing that something is wrong. But it's too late. I've already regained enough strength to call forth the darkness that has been lurking in my powerhouse ever since Aunt Miriam willed it to me. I'm ready, willing, and even looking forward to killing her, which is what activates it. The black ink travels up, flowing into my irises.

My upper lip curls up, my gums harden, and my teeth sharpen.

"What in the cursed realms," the Sea Witch shrieks as she watches my appearance change.

I speak the special dark spell, and will the fire of Tartarus to ignite under her black octopus skin. It starts in her tentacles.

She thrashes around, struggling to put out a fire she can't even see. As she twists and turns like a stabbed snake I get up to my feet, walking around her.

"I'm using this power for the first time." I look down at her like a dark queen. "So I'm not very skilled with it, which means I could kill you without actually intending to. So be careful with your reactions, don't give me reason to flare—pun intended."

I tone down the fire, and step in front of her. "Listen, Ursula, and listen well. I have the power to burn you with Tartarus fire from the inside out, do you know what that means? It means that you'd become a vassal of the underworld, with me as your mistress. I could control you like a voodoo doll. My power would work on you only at night, but any attempt to harm me or free yourself of me during the day would be punished harshly after sundown, through this burning pain you're experiencing now. Not to mention that I could send you on suicide missions, or condition you to torture yourself."

"But how can this be?" She cries. "You're the descendant of Poseidon, not a creature of the underworld."

"I would have expected more consideration of the variables from the ancient Sea Witch. You see, my grandmother—you know, the nymph who got that old bastard of a king to ask for her hand in marriage—she was forced to marry another man in the human world, someone who could keep her safe. Turns out that someone was none other than Hades."

"No, it can't be."

"As you can see, it can. Seems you were right about my grandmother. There was something special about her that got the most powerful men, gods no less, to fall for her. She had a daughter with Hades. My Aunt Miriam. Who inherited this dark power, and now passed it on to me. Zillard being Hades' son as well, I suppose our signatures are quite similar."

She hisses and attacks, launching herself at me like a snake. Instinctively, I move out of her way, and she tumbles on her own weight, but she gets back up quickly.

"Stupid girl," she hisses. "I've been around for thousands of years. I looked Death in the face so many times it's grown tired of me. You wouldn't be able to destroy me if you were made of Hades' very rib."

She waves her hand, and telekinetic force smacks me in the chest. It throws me across the cave, my back slamming into the cave wall. It knocks the air from my lungs, and I fall down on all fours. By the time I get a grip again, the Sea Witch has already gotten to me, now standing on her tentacles again. She grabs me with one around my throat, and pins me to the wall.

This is what it must feel like to have a snake around your neck, strangling you. My face swells, and darkness starts to creep at the corners of my vision. I can't reach my powers anymore, which means she's strangling them, too, through my body.

"The only thing that you've accomplished with this show is that I won't take the time to put you through different kinds of almost-deaths. Take this as a blessing, that you'll die quicker than I originally planned."

Which means that at least now she's afraid of me, and won't give me a chance to attack her again. My head is swelling, my mind clouding as darkness closes in on the Sea Witch's face. As she's always desired, hers is the face I'll see right before I die. But at the last moment it transforms into another face. God, I hadn't realized how deeply I craved to see him.

Lysander. His ice blue eyes are charged with the intensity he showed when we last saw each other. The same longing. His sharp warrior features change as he raises his hand and brushes a tear off my cheek. I didn't even realize I was crying.

I run my fingers through his long, golden hair that feels like silk, and finally close my eyes, letting the mating bond permeate me, and smooth my passing.

"*I will always be with you,*" he whispers in my head.

Arielle

A CRASH RIPS THROUGH the air, and fire bursts in my lungs. I find myself on all fours, on the ground, the Sea Witch cursing like a mad woman somewhere close. Beside me, a flashing blade embedded in the rock, and a severed tentacle.

I spot the Sea Witch, howling, her face distorted with pain. Tiny red vessels crisscross the whites of her eyes.

"You," she snarls, baring her fangs at Lysander.

Lysander. My heart slams into my chest. The mates' bond between us, that's how he must have found me, like last time.

He's standing on a platform above us, looking like a god in his armor. His gaze meets mine, and our bond lights up like a neural pathway between us, filling my heart with an unbearable affection.

The Sea Witch grabs me, with her hands this time, holding me in front of her like a shield. She puts a piece of chipped iron to my throat.

"Come down here and drop your weapons, or I'll kill her," she snarls, spittle landing on the side of my face. She stinks badly of stale black magic.

Lysander jumps down from the platform, landing with a thud on the ground, dust rising from under his feet. He rises to his full height, looking sleek and deadly.

"I cannot drop my weapons, Sea Witch, because I *am* my weapons." He opens his gauntleted hand, and a blade takes form out of thin air, showing her that his weapons are made of his own flesh, like his mail. It glints sharply, the same color as his armor. "But don't worry," he continues, "because I won't be fighting you."

"No, you won't fight me. You'll surrender to me. You'll take a blood oath to serve me whenever I call upon you, if you want your protégé back."

"I can't make a blood oath to you. I already bound myself to someone else, to serve as man *and* as warrior."

One glance is enough to understand he means me. He can't be acting, not in a situation of life or death, like this one. Can he?

"Then your little princess is coming with me." She starts retreating. "If you came with warriors, tell them to stand down, or I'll slit her pretty throat."

"I didn't come with anybody, but I didn't come alone either. And I didn't come to kill you, but neither to let you live."

"No, it would seem you're here to battle me in riddles, King of Frost."

I struggle against the witch, but my body is exhausted from the struggle, the wounds and the healing process, I'm too weak. I try to conjure my darkness, but I'm too weak for that, too.

The Sea Witch looks around for hidden warriors, losing her cool. I glance around for magic, dark mist or the rippling air caused by invisible beings, but then I begin to feel it.

The silver drawings start to move under my skin. They glow, emerge to the surface of my body, and then peel off like dead skin. I stare in awe at them and then at Lysander, noticing his lips move.

By the highest realms—he's releasing my powers. They start to boil in my powerhouse, until they feel like rising waves. The sound of the sea outside turns into a roar. It feels me, too, it wants to bond with me. I abandon myself against the Sea Witch's body, my mind opening to understand her on the most profound levels—the sea gives me that power; in the end, the Sea Witch is her child. She might be the villain in my life now, but she's meaningful to the sea. I know I have to kill her but, surprisingly, I know I won't be enjoying it.

I turn in her grip. I can see myself in her eyes now. I'm no longer made of flesh, My body is shifting into the water girl, which is why I was able to slip from her arms.

"Thank you," I whisper to her, and I mean it. She's done so much service for the sea, I can feel it in every one of my water cells.

Ursula the Sea Witch stares at me in awe, and I hope she feels how hard this is for me.

My powers mount, my body becoming completely made of water. I retain my human shape, but little else of my human condition. Slowly, with respect, I open Ursula's mouth with my hands. She gives in easily, as if hypnotized by me. Acting on instinct that feels more like ancient wisdom, I descend head first into her mouth, and flood her body in my water form.

Basically, I'm drowning her.

But she doesn't offer resistance. She opens her mind to me, and I understand—to her, it feels like sacrificing herself to a goddess.

"*Killing me doesn't solve your real problem,*" she speaks in my mind. "*Xerxes will never stop hunting you.*"

"*Xerxes' fate is already sealed.*"

"*Don't underestimate him. Some say he is invincible.*"

"*And it's almost true. Almost.*" I reveal the secret that Zillard showed me at the lake, the secret weapon that will lead to Xerxes' demise. It mirrors in the Sea Witch's mind, and she smiles.

She takes a few moments as if to bask in the sensation of me flowing through her system. The last thing she says before her soul dissipates into the water is, "*Your Majesty.*"

And I feel honored. It means a lot that, before she died, the Sea Witch acknowledged me as her princess, royalty of the ocean. And that is exactly how I feel as I reform in the cave, my body still made of water. I spread my arms and lift my face, enjoying the feeling of complete liberation. I can feel the ocean outside roar for me, demanding that I let it embrace me.

Then I feel *them*. The trapped spirits of my family, dissolving in the air with a collective, echoing sigh, as if perfect pleasure courses through them. With the Sea Witch dead, they've been freed from their deformed bodies, which served as prison for their spirits. What an awful fate she gave them—and how much she must have suffered after Poseidon stabbed her in the back; she was in love with him, I know that now. It had been her grief that turned her evil, but she'd been evil for so long, it couldn't be reversed.

"Arielle." It's Lysander, his voice like cream on my senses. Since now I don't hear with my ears nor see with my eyes, I can feel the essence of him.

I face him. There's no more lying now. In this shape, I can see through him, but his aura turns opaque in an instant.

"You won't reveal your secrets to me, King of Frost," I say in a voice that I barely recognize. It's musical, and fluid, a little deeper than in my human form. "Anything particular you prefer to keep hidden?"

He suddenly jumps in front of me, his blade blocking the attack of a walking shark with the snout like a sabre. The creature isn't alone. Dozens pour in from dark tunnels connected to the cave—the Sea Witch's minions, thirsty for revenge.

"Run, go, now!" Lysander urges me, swinging his blade expertly, blocking and slicing the beasts in half as they appear.

But the power in my veins won't let me back down. I open my arms, close my eyes, and call on the ocean.

"It's time you and I finally united," I whisper, inviting roaring waves into the cave. They swerve around Lysander, but hit the beasts head on. As the sea washes them away, I can feel it take complete control over my body. It's like holding the reins of a carriage that goes too fast, the speed dizzying, and the wheels breaking against holes.

"Lysander," I whisper, reaching out to him for help. My hands are already starting to lose their shape, turning into a fingerless mass. "I'm losing my body," I cry, my voice turning into the sound of a cascade. "I can't contain it, Lysander, please."

I'm becoming one with the ocean. My power is claiming me.

He hurries close, and looks down at me with so much intensity in his blue eyes, that I start to feel my heart again. My heart that beats harder and harder, tormented by questions—what does he really feel for me? Does the mates' bond really have an effect on him, or did he really only play with me all along? No matter the answers, these feelings make me feel human again. So does his touch.

He closes his eyes, his palms growing hotter on a part of my body that I identify as the sides of my torso. He's balancing me out, helping me contain my power. I gasp as water turns to flesh, not by far as painfully as the first two times, but by the time the transformation is done, I fall into his arms, exhausted, and barely knowing who I am.

CHAPTER VII

Arielle

A log fire glows warmly on my cheek. I curl under a thick duvet that seems made of furs, blinking up at Lysander's face. He's stroking my forehead gently with his finger.

"I was afraid I lost you," he murmurs, his voice like a caress. I smile, lost in this vision of him, but then a flash of memory hits me. I sit up, pain shooting through my body.

"The Pearl of Riches. We lost it. Damn it, all this has been for nothing!"

But Lysander holds up the familiar shabby shell, between two strong fingers. "I swiped it off the ground when I jumped from the platform," he explains with a smile. God, will I ever be able to look away from those beautiful lips? Will I ever be able to remain detached when his icy features change to express the warmest emotions?

No, I won't let him do this. He's only manipulating me. I reach for the memory of what I saw in the demon eye, him telling Minerva how he was only pretending to be in love in order to control me, and then how he scooped her up and took her to the bed. I push myself further away from him, pulling my knees up.

"Thank you for saving me," I say dryly. "I wish I could say I had it under control, but I totally didn't. You saved my life. But then again, you almost took it a few times, too."

A shadow falls over his face. Whether it's sadness, frustration or even fury, I don't know, but it looks scary. Still, I won't back down, I won't start to make excuses for him. I look away, at our surroundings, realizing we're inside a cave. He must have teleported us from the Sea Witch's lair.

"Why are we hiding here? Why didn't you take me back to the castle, or the Seelie?"

"Your body wasn't strong enough to withstand a long teleportation. We're in the rocky mountains by the sea, a few miles from where the Sea Witch kept you."

A snowstorm rages outside, but the sound only reaches us faintly. The cold not at all.

"I formed a protective shield," Lysander explains, his voice deep and dark. I become suddenly aware that I'm naked under the furs, my rags drying by the fire.

"Can I have my outfit back, please? I'd rather wear wet rags than the fur of murdered animals."

"These furs come from monster shifters, creatures that lure stray supernaturals in the mountains and feast on them. They're not the puppies and bears you know from your world."

He gets up and walks over to a pile of wood. He must have gathered it while I was out. He moves with the grace of a killer. Everything about him is deadly, and metallic, and feral.

"What was happening when I contacted you telepathically?" I inquire as he returns with wood for the fire. "I heard the sounds of battle."

"Yes, there was an ambush. Just outside the Seelie Fae realm. Xerxes sent a unit of stray demons and serpent shifters, but we managed to push them back."

"Stray demons? Does that mean that Xerxes has got Lucifer on his side?" I can't hide the alarm in my voice.

"No, he wouldn't take sides in this. But some creatures from hell escape and act of their own accord, that's why we call them stray. They're sort of like mercenaries." He opens a sash by my drying clothes, and hands me a fluffy, delicious looking piece of fae bread.

Only now do I realize how hungry I was. I snatch it from his hand and sink my teeth in it, moaning when I feel the taste.

"Oh, God," I whisper in delight. "I never get tired of this smell." Not to mention that it will provide me with more nutrients than any meal in the human world.

I watch Lysander as he works the fire. My eyes skim over his profile and his body, willing myself not to find him painfully handsome. Crap, I need to distract myself ASAP.

"If you help me balance my power long term, control and wield it properly," I say, "I promise I'll share it with you. Even if you're marrying Minerva, I will still stand by your side. I will use my powers to fight against Xerxes, and I'll yield to you command of the seas when you need them. All I ask is that you let me keep my power, and teach me how to use it."

But instead of smiling satisfied, Lysander's face becomes grimmer. The flames cast their glow over his blue eyes, making him resemble a beautiful devil. His strong jaw sharpens so much it could splinter rocks.

"Are you also willing to swear that you'll never marry another man, and share your power with him by being intimate with him?"

"No, wait a minute, you don't get to make that kind of demands on me. This is the part where you take my hand, look deep into my eyes and tell me how amazing I am for agreeing to put my power in your service, even though you're marrying Minerva."

"Oh, yes, it is amazing that you're ready to accept my marriage with Minerva so serenely. I'm thrilled."

"There's no way around that marriage, Lysander, so what's your problem?"

"What's my problem?" His eyes flash at me. "I'll tell you. This isn't you being generous and forgiving, Arielle. This is you opening the way for a relationship with Zillard Dark. You're in love with him." He snarls like an animal, his eyes bloodshot. The gauntlet coats his fist in a flash before he slams it into the rock wall, tearing a chunk out of it.

"What's gotten into you, Lysander, calm down."

"Oh, you want me to calm down? You shroud yourself in the warlock's shadows and lose yourself with him in the Seelie gardens, and you want me to calm down? We have a mates' bond, for fuck's sake! My blood is inside you. I am yours, and you're mine, whether either of us wants to or not. You think you can just leave me, like some kind of holiday fling?"

"Cut the charade, Lysander." I hold a finger in his face, my eyes burning into his. "You are the one who never honored that bond. You only used it to chain me to you, to strip me of my options. I saw you with Minerva in your room, I saw you grab her ass and rock your cock against her." I grow more furious from the image in my head. "I heard what you told her about me. I know the passion in your eyes isn't real. You've only been using it to make me believe I mattered to you. But you would never take me seriously, mates' bond or not."

Tears stream down my face as all the frustration and pent up rage find release. Before I know it I've thrown off the furs and launched myself naked at Lysander. I hit his chest with my fists, screaming my frustration and pain at being used and rejected.

What's baffling is that he doesn't even try to stop me. On the contrary, his defenses go down, his armor fading against his body. He's now standing naked in front of me, my fists landing against his steel hard pecs. They hurt so bad I have to stop. Slowly, gently, he wraps his big hands around my wrists.

"I often think about what your life would have been like, if I'd never taken you from the human world," he says in a voice that caresses me like velvet. Holding my hands in a light grip, he brushes my hair behind my ear with the other, looking at me like I'm the most precious thing in the world. "If you'd never used magic, or if I'd never found out. Or if I'd simply decided not to uproot you. You would have finished your studies. Enjoyed a career and morning take-away at Starbucks. Girls' nights and bachelorette parties. Maybe limos and cocktails and, later when married a former quarterback and had a couple of kids."

I try to pull away, scared of the way I'm falling under his spell.

"Lysander, what are you—"

But he keeps me close. "If you only knew what those scenarios do to me whenever I play them in my mind, Arielle." He sounds so tormented that tears swell in my eyes. His hand splays over the small of my back, pressing me to him. "Tell me the truth. Did you make love to Zillard Dark? Did you give yourself to him?"

I shake my head like I can't believe the question, even though I intentionally planted these doubts in his mind. I wanted the possibility to torment him, the way his relationship with Minerva tortured me. But Zillard is like a brother to me.

Lysander's embrace turns to steel around me.

"Just tell me. Don't prolong this uncertainty."

"I've never been with any man, Lysander," I say as my breasts crush against the hard sinews of his body. We're both naked, vulnerable, facing one another without defenses. His eyes mirror the fire's glow, highlighting his passion.

"Swear to me," he says. "Swear to me he never touched you."

"My word is not enough?"

"Maybe he used his incubus powers to seduce you, and you're trying to protect him from me." He caresses my chin with two strong fingers that feel like weapons. "Because you know that, if he did that, I would skin him alive, and put salt all over him."

I cab feel he's capable of that and more, and I shudder.

"The idea bothers you?" he rumbles.

I take a deep breath, hoping he'll take my next words for what they are—the truth. "Zillard is like a brother to me. His father Hades, is Aunt Miriam's father as well. When she willed her power to me, Zillard and I became, how shall I put it—siblings, somehow."

Lysander looks deeply into my eyes as he processes the information, and his features begin to relax.

"You, on the other hand, you have no excuse for anything you did." I say grimly. "You slept with Minerva. You told her that your feelings for me weren't real."

"Arielle—"

"No. Don't give me white lies, because they aren't going to work. These are things I've seen with my own eyes, and heard with my own ears, there's no way you can reframe that so that I believe you. I just want to know—How were you able to bind yourself to me, and yet love another woman? Because—" And here comes the hard part. "I don't think I'll ever be able to love another man."

There's so much passion in his eyes, it's almost murderous.

"You belong to me, Arielle." His voice rumbles deep in his chest as his hand travels up my naked back. He cups the nape of my neck possessively, his lips dangerously close. I can feel he has a hard time controlling himself. "Whether we like it or not, we *are* bonded. You and I will forever crave each other, no matter what."

"You're marrying Minerva," I remind him, struggling with the fire in my lower belly. "You and I, we can't be, unless you call off the engagement."

"I would do it without a second thought if it didn't put you at risk. Minerva would have you killed. Remember the man who spoke against you at the meeting? Mage Igarus, who suggested we should end your life?"

"How can I forget." The need for revenge surges through at the memory, and I try to push myself away for Lysander. But he yanks me back to him.

"Minerva had him speak out against you. And that was just her warming up."

"You said you'd thought about killing me yourself, you bastard." I struggle in his arms.

"You know why I said it, deep down you always knew." Fire casts a glow of madness over his irises. "I had to make it all credible, I had to make Minerva think you really didn't matter to me, so she'd leave you alone."

"So everything you did—Stating in front of anyone that I mattered so little to you you'd watch me die without a problem, telling Minerva you only act like you have feelings for me in order to manipulate me, everything that transpired was a plot?"

"Yes. And yes. Here."

He lets me go and steps back from me, grabbing an iron dagger he must have brought from the Sea Witch's lair.

"I took this in case we came across Fire Fae, but let's give it another purpose." He takes the iron dagger to his chest, and slashes his left pec. I shriek when blood swells out, and the skin around the cut starts to turn black like burning paper in an instant.

"No, don't hurt yourself," I cry. It must hurt like hell, but Lysander doesn't even grimace. With intensity in his eyes, he drops the dagger, steps close, and cups my face.

"Lick my blood."

"What? No!"

"It will reveal to you my true feelings and intentions. It will give you a glimpse of my true heart."

Can I be so selfish to take his blood only to discover his true feelings? Use it like some sort of twisted means of divination? I don't know, but his blood is streaming out of his wound, weakening him because he cut himself with iron. If I touch him there, I can heal him.

I rise on my toes and touch my tongue to the thick trail of blood, sending my healing power into his body. Without it, the wound would take weeks to heal, and it would weaken his entire organism in the process.

His blood feels warm, but tastes of snow and winter. My lids close, and my eyes roll back—his blood permeates my heart. I feel what he feels for me, and the main emotion is jealousy. Hundreds of scenarios spin in his mind of me choosing another man. I feel the torture in his heart whenever he saw me even smile at another. I disengage, the power of his feelings overwhelming.

When I open my eyes and meet Lysander's, I can't resist anymore. I jump on him, closing my naked legs around his hips.

I crush my mouth against his, my arms tight around his neck. He opens his mouth, groaning with pleasure.

"Finally, I get to feel you," he says, opening his mouth against mine. He pushes his tongue between my lips, gently like the brush of a feather, to make sure it's not too much too quickly, but he grows demanding within seconds.

I give in to his desire as he lays me down on the furs by the fire, our bodies burning with lust as we undulate into each other. He parts my knees with his. Is he actually getting ready to take me? Are Lysander and I finally going to make love?

I squirm, inviting him to take me, as he bends down to kiss my neck, sending ribbons of pleasure all through me.

"Ah, Lysander," I whisper, relishing in the sensation. I have fooled around with guys before in the mortal world, back when I didn't even suspect what the future held for me, but never have I felt like this. The way my skin reacts to him is new, and quite frankly alarming.

He moves down to my chest and my breasts, taking his time loving them, his muscles glistening in the firelight. I'm so wet down there, my cream slips to my inner thighs. I won't be able to resist him if he goes on kissing my body possessively, while the flames cast that beautiful glow on his skin.

"Lysander, if we do this—"

But I can't even finish the sentence. He moves swiftly up and pins my hands above my head, his gaze wild with desire.

"I have never wanted a woman like this, Arielle, never." He slides his steel-hard cock between my folds, over my clit. I arch up my chest, aching with need. "True, I've never been bonded to one either. But I never expected it would feel this way."

I open my legs wider, lifting my hips to meet his big cock as it glides between my folds. He hisses, his eyelids hooding his bright blue eyes, his lip curling over his teeth. God, he looks like a magnificent predator enjoying his prey.

"If I give you my virtue now, my virginity," I whisper, craving to caress his artwork of a body, "Will you set me free? Will you go back to your Minerva, and let me restart my life with someone new, wipe out the painful past?"

His irises flash with a murderous impulse, only not against me—against the man I might be referring to. He ruts me harder, our bodies hungry for each other as we writhe on the furs by the fire. I can tell he's struggling to contain himself and not plunge into me.

"Never," he grunts. "Any man who dares make a move on you will die, remember that. I'll sneak in the shadows behind their backs and snap their necks, and that would be me being merciful."

I smile—just what I wanted to hear. I lift my chin, inviting him to kiss me, and he takes the chance like a madman.

I would like to let my hands travel down to his powerful buttocks, clasp them and feel those steel muscles move, but he keeps my hands above my head.

"Stick it inside of me, Lysander," I whisper, feverish with need.

"Stick what?" he provokes. "Say it."

"Your cock, King of Frost. I want your cock fucking me, and sealing the bond we have with each other forever."

He pushes the head of his mighty cock between my folds. The wide crest of his cock parts my walls, making my whole body tense up.

"Relax," he slurs. "I'll be gentle. I want you to love this." With that, he pushes it just a little harder, his mighty cock urging against the flimsy barrier of my virginity.

"By the cursed realms, so warm and sleek." His deep voice rumbles as he pushes again, and it's like a red iron piercing me. My wrists strain against his hold.

He moves, slowly, the pain subsiding. It's a delicious ache that makes me crave more. Lysander buries his face into he curve of my neck, kissing me with lust.

"This is a first for me as well, my forbidden love," he whispers hotly in my ear. "I have never been with a virgin before."

I look up at the cave ceiling, the flames playing wildly against the rock. I push my hips forward to meet his next move, and kiss his earlobe lovingly. He raises his face surprised, his intense gaze meeting mine. I lift my head as much as his hold on my wrists allows, and lick his neck, loving his taste of winter and arctic wind on my tongue. He groans, thrusting hard, making me cry out.

"Forgive me," he says hotly, resting his forehead against mine, struggling to contain himself. I push my breasts into his chest, feeling the blood from his wound dripping from his chest onto mine. The need to become one with him overwhelms me.

"Let go of my hands, Lysander," I ask him sweetly.

He releases my wrists, and I use the opportunity to quickly slit my wrist with my fingernail. All I've managed to cause is a small cut that only gives out a few drops of blood before he catches my hand, not having expected this.

"Arielle, why are you hurting yourself?"

"You've made a blood oath to me," I muse. "But I never made one to you. So here I am, doing it."

"No."

"Why not?"

"If you give me your blood and make a blood oath, you will feel about me as strongly as I feel about you. And that's...slow death on the inside. Every second of separation is like walking with a blade thrust between your ribs."

"I know. You gave me a glimpse into your feelings, remember?" I look at the slanting slash on his left pec.

"I know I'm not doing the right thing, Lysander, but I know what I want—to be yours; forever. I want to be the only woman with a true claim on you."

He bends his head to kiss me, his long blond hair brushing the side of my face, but I put my wrist between us.

"This right here, King of Frost," I whisper, "this moment is sublimely intimate. It's more than holy ground could ever be. You're inside of me, by a fire that matches my passion for you. Lysander, let me be yours forever."

"You feel passion for me," he whispers, rocking his big cock into me. It parts my walls more, making way, but it doesn't feel quite as uncomfortable as the first time.

"I crave you more than anything," I plead truthfully. "Take my blood, and make me yours. Let us be one."

He can't resist, and closes his hot lips on the little wound on my wrist. He sucks gently, and when the taste of my blood hits his taste buds, his eyes flash to mine. It feels like he can see into the darkest depths of my soul. We're connecting on the deepest level.

He moves inside me, slowly, carefully, enjoying the sensations my body is giving him. We lose ourselves in each other as we make love, Lysander thrusting harder as I grow more comfortable with him.

Soon we're panting, our sweating bodies sliding on each other, the scent of sex filling the cave, and driving us even wilder. Lysander closes his eyes as his mouth disengages from my wrist. He leans his head back as he takes in the pleasure and our connection, his golden hair flowing to his powerful shoulders. Shoulders that I crave to touch.

I hold on tightly to them as I build up, the tension inside my core threatening to explode.

He thrusts into me, now unbridled. I can't believe that I'm about to have an orgasm, my first time. This isn't normal, women don't come the first time they make love, do they?

But climax keeps mounting in my body as I watch this beautiful beast claiming me. I explode around him, my fingers turning white as they clench on his rock-hard upper arms. My head swims from the exquisite sensations.

Lysander spills his seed inside of me. I can feel it flooding my pussy, his cock throbbing against my walls. God, he fills me so good. He empties himself inside of me, bucking and swearing in the most sinful way. When he lies on the fur by my side he's breathing hard, still inside of me. He rolls me over him, so that I'm straddling him now, and it feels amazing. He kisses me with so much love that I become submissive in his arms.

"I can't believe this actually happened," I say with a smile, my lips deliciously swollen from his kisses.

We spend long moments staring at each other. He's so incredibly beautiful lying on the furs, his golden hair spread around his head, his warrior features now relaxed, and his ice blue eyes lost in mine. I trace his sharp cheekbones with my finger, drinking him in without even trying to hide it.

"What is it?" he whispers, brushing my hair behind my ear.

"You're so beautiful, Lysander. And I can't believe I just had you, that you were the first man in my life."

The flames rustle, and his eyes turn savage. He wraps his impossibly strong arms around me.

"Not just the first. The *only* man."

I try to move, because this doesn't feel like the right position to have this conversation, but he doesn't let me. He opens his big hand over my loins, pushing gently while also lifting his hips, so that I can get an even better feel of his still hard cock filling me.

"You. Are. Mine," he says with a low growl. "And I am yours. Bonded mates are for eternity. We don't get to separate even in the afterlife, you know that?"

Sadness washes over me.

"Then that's when we'll be together. In this world, you belong to Minerva, you pledged yourself to her."

"You know damn well why I did it, and so does she. My union with Minerva isn't based on love, it never has been. I could never feel for her what I feel for you."

"Is that so?" Hearing that does something to me. I start rocking my hips, riding him. Surprise changes the hard planes of his face. "What about the time when you had sex with her in your chamber?"

"What are you talking about, Arielle, I never had sex with her." His breath goes short as I move in sensual circles on his cock, running my hands over his fantastic body.

"I saw it in the demon eye—"

"The demon eye," he cuts me off, trying to make me still down. But I ride him faster, wanting to punish him for having been with another woman, subduing him. I will make him com, groaning. But he manages to resist, though his sharp cheeks heat up.

"You clearly didn't watch everything," he manages in a husky voice. "If you had, you'd know I dropped her on the bed when I saw the demon eye between the pillows. I asked her what she thought she was doing, and she swore by all realms that she hadn't planted it there."

I keep circling my hips on him, his muscles cording up.

"And you believed her?"

"No. I knew she'd set it all up so you would watch. So I dropped her on the bed and asked her to leave. Still, I pretended to believe her. I didn't want her to know I saw through her schemes."

I don't know what to say. Only the rustling of the fire fills the silence between us.

He cups my breasts, touching them as if in worship before sliding his hands down my body and grabbing my hips.

"I never betrayed you, Arielle." His gaze fills with animal lust. "And now that I've been inside of you, I will never respond to another woman again. In fact, my body didn't respond to Minerva that day, either. I had to think about you to get it up."

I sense the truth of that statement, which drives me crazy with lust. I rock on him, the juices of my pleasure coating him, my moans filling the cave. Lysander struggles to resist his orgasm, to prolong my delight.

I reach behind me, and take his balls in my hand. They're wet from my cream. Lysander's cock pulses inside me, I feel him so deep now that it hurts. But I love the pain. I come, screaming his name.

"I won't stay away from you, Lysander, even if it costs me my life."

Lysander

FAE LINE THE ROAD TO the Seelie King's castle, their cheers rising to the sky. Since Xerxes' ambush outside their realm, my warriors and I haven't been back, so this is a delayed celebration. Xerxes hadn't known that I was here with part of my Court, and his attack had been meant to ambush and assassinate the Seelie King, to make sure he doesn't take my side in this war.

Bad decision. The Seelie King had wanted to stay neutral, but now he's pissed.

I'm all too aware of Arielle's presence on the back of a white unicorn behind me. I can feel her breathing, her heart beating steadily, her scent of sea and fresh breeze wafting to my nostrils. In this beautiful landscape of the Seelie realm, with the fairy dust and magic nature all around, she's happy. She takes it all in, and I know she'd like to stay here. It hurts all the more that I have to take her with me back to the rock castle by the ocean. A lot to take care of, prepare for war.

The grand gates open to the castle'a inner courtyard. Army, civilians, and noble members of the Seelie Court throw flowers and magic in the air, cheering for their saviors. But I barely manage to smile, knowing what's waiting for me in the grand hall—separation from Arielle. Thinking about is like being crucified.

"King of Frost," Calabriel Seawrath greets with open arms as we step into the grand hall. The noble members of the Seelie Court and Army have been asked to remain outside, so that only Arielle and I enter. The doors close behind us, and two of Minerva's guards stomp over to Arielle. Instead of properly greeting Minerva, Calabriel, and the Seelie King, I turn sharply to the guards.

"Do not touch her."

"But you lifted the silver spell, and freed her powers," Minerva says calmly, but I hear the poison behind her words. "She could be dangerous, to us and to herself, if she doesn't master them right."

"I'm here to balance her out." One look at my half brother Sandros is enough for him to take a protective stance by Arielle's side. "Besides, we are going to train her to use her powers, and she will be aiding us in the war against Xerxes. I think we should start treating her with the respect owed to a fae of her standing."

"Half fae," Minerva blocks viciously, her icy eyes shooting daggers at Arielle.

"So it's true, her powers have been restored," Calabriel says in his oily tone. The thin layer of slime on his face glints in the sunlight that floods the hall through the great arched windows. "But she will not claim her throne as ruler of the Sea Court, yes? As promised?"

Until Arielle answers, I can hear the worry in Calabriel's breathing.

"She will not claim the throne," Arielle finally replies. Relief pours out with Calabriel's next breath. "And we have brought you the Pearl of Riches." She holds it out, but doesn't approach him. If he wants it, Calabriel will have to go to her.

When he does, it makes me smile in the corner of my mouth. He's scared of her unrestrained powers, afraid she might use them to finish him. He basically snatches the Pearl from her hand, and returns quickly to where he'd been standing with Minerva and the Seelie King, crouched greedily over the item he holds in his hands.

Minerva lifts her chin, keeping her hands laced together in front of her like some wronged saint.

"I would have expected a warmer greeting," she says to me.

I walk over to her. I can feel all eyes on us, but I can't even pretend anymore. Yesterday I claimed Arielle like a beast in a cave, the taste of her still lingers in my mouth. I wouldn't be able to fake a relationship with Minerva anymore even if I wanted to.

And Minerva sees it in my eyes. I can tell by the way her expression changes. I can't hide my true feelings for Arielle anymore, and I can only hope that Minerva understands that. We have a moment here, one in which I almost expect her to set me free from our arrangement. After all, it was never about love. From my part, not even about lust, and she knows it. But just as I'm getting my hopes up that she'll understand, Calabriel bursts into laughter.

We all turn to him. He's laughing like a mad man that just discovered the way to fulfill all his wishes as he holds the glinting pearl in the sun. He's taken it out of the shabby shell.

"The Pearl of Riches," he calls enthusiastically, "and the Sea Court, mine to command." He looks right at Minerva, and that look speaks volumes. It's like he's telling her, "*Don't you wish you hadn't dumped me now?*"

But Minerva groans, almost imperceptibly, and rolls her eyes. Poor guy never really stood a chance. She only fucked him for the beauty he once possessed, and then she plagued him with bad emotions that robbed him of it. I almost pity him.

"Now it's time that you honor your side of the bargain. Fight alongside us against Xerxes, and bring in your allies from the human world." During the ambush outside of the realm, he didn't even move a finger, he just lounged here, waiting for the Pearl. I'll make sure to put him in the front line first chance I get.

"Of course," he replies. "A deal is a deal." He gives us a slimy grin. Then he raises his voice, as if there were a roaring crowd in here, eager to drink every word from his lips. "In fact, I just got the best idea possible. We could make this an unbreakable alliance, and that way you would never doubt my loyalty again."

He looks to Arielle, my beautiful mate. She stands there, dressed in an emerald gown, looking breathtakingly gorgeous. I white-knuckle the hilt of my dagger as Calabriel's eyes travel over her like she's a trophy.

"Give me Arielle's hand in marriage, and I will remain your vassal for eternity."

Fury makes my ears whistle. Is he doing this in order to piss me off, or because he's greedy for all the advantages that come from being intimate with her, like wielding the ocean's powers, or is he trying to make Minerva jealous?

Minerva laughs and steps down from the royal dais.

"What a fabulous idea, Calabriel," she says, placing a hand on his shoulder. He looks like he wants to shake it off, but refrains.

Arielle looks from one to the other confused. "You're kidding, right? Who's to force me to marry you?" She looks at Calabriel like a queen, and he takes notice.

"Nobody can give you Arielle," I put in as I descend from the dais and approach them. "Nobody has the right to decide her fate."

"But you're her guardian."

I could slap the idiot.

"Are you stupid, or are you just pretending?" Arielle says. "I risked my life to get you the Pearl of Riches. I killed the Sea Witch and escaped her minions, I have powers from both Poseidon and Hades. I've proven that I'm perfectly capable of taking care of myself, so Lysander is no longer my guardian. We stick together because we have a common goal, but he cannot decide over me."

"She's right," I say.

"You—" Calabriel points to Arielle, his words almost a threat. "Need to be part of a Court, sweet girl.

You stick with Lysander Nightfrost because you trust him more than others, I understand, but you are *not* part of his Court. Even if we annihilate Xerxes, you'll always require protection. Being on your own in the supernatural world, with no clan, no Court, no coven, no nothing to support you, it's suicide. And you are an asset many desire." He tries to take her hand, but she jerks it away.

One could cut the tension in the great hall with a knife. Fae cheer outside, waiting for their king, Calabriel and I to appear on the balcony and officially announce the Sea Witch's defeat. She was a villain the supernatural world had been hunting down for a long time. Also, they can't wait for us to officially present Arielle.

"It's time," the Seelie King interrupts gently, and we all head towards the balcony, the cheers outside turning louder.

It angers me that we have to display her like a trophy weapon. Now that it's come out who she truly is, they want to see as much as possible of the daughter of the ocean, who also wields dark powers straight out of Tartarus. She is an asset indeed, but she is also so vulnerable that it moves me to tears.

Flowers and magic shoot up in the sky, spring scents wafting on the air.

"Think about my proposal," Calabriel says to Arielle, while smiling down at the crowd. "It would give you power over the Sea Court. This means I would be sharing the throne with you."

"Bring that into discussion again," Arielle retorts sharply, "and I will raise the entire ocean over you."

There's no mistaking what Calabriel wants—he wants to share her powers. He wants to command the ocean, and that can only be done by making love to Arielle. But no man is ever going to touch her, I will kill each and every one that sets his eyes on her, even if that makes me a serial killer.

Calabriel retreats from the balcony, now that his retinue is here to escort him.

"Time for me to return to my Court, and prepare for the upcoming war," he says. "We might not get much time." After he takes his leave from us, he turns one last time to Arielle. "Make no mistake, daughter of the ocean," he says with the sly look of a fox. "By the time this is over, you will be my bride. Even if I have to force you."

Lysander

"YOU'RE IN LOVE WITH her," Minerva spits in anger, following me to my chamber and slamming the door shut. "I saw it in the way you looked at Calabriel after he said he'd claim her as his bride, so don't even try to deny it."

When I don't reply she runs after me, and grabs my arm, forcing me to turn around, just as my armor fades from my body.

"Minerva, I've just come back from a mission that's been draining and exhausting. I need an ice bath, and time to rest. I can't deal with this right now."

"You're drained from fucking her. I could smell you on each other, you bastard." She slaps her palms against my chest, her gold and silver hair a mess, thin red veins crisscrossing the whites of her eyes. It stirs pity in my heart. I have to tell her the truth, I owe her that much.

"You're right. I took Arielle to the rocky mountains after the Sea Witch was defeated. I only wanted to let her rest, and then bring her back. But things rarely happen how we plan them. I couldn't resist her."

"That tramp, she used her powers to seduce you."

"What? No. I have been into her the entire time, Minerva. I lied to you, and maybe also to myself, when I said I was only pretending. Somewhere along the way those feelings became real." They have been real all along, but the look of hurt on Minerva's face prompts me to sugarcoat that. It would cause her too much pain. Even if the only thing that hurts is probably her ego.

"She did," she insists, looking like a mad woman, holding a finger in my face. "She used her water nymph powers on you, messed with your head."

"Minerva, you're in denial."

"She used her love spells. She's more powerful now, with her sea magic activated, and with whatever darkness has seeped inside her from her aunt. You couldn't resist her, that's why your feelings for her intensified over time."

"Minerva." I put my hands around her shoulders, trying to ground her somehow, help her accept reality for what it is. "I. Love. Her. And it's real.."

We hold each other's gaze for long moments.

"I think we should call our engagement off," I say, keeping my tone soft. "I know, it's unprecedented among our kind, we're pledged to each other, and it's known around all the supernatural realms. But everybody knows it wasn't about love between us, it was about strategic alliance. An alliance that you, too, have an interest in. You know it's best for you and your people to stay."

She folds her arms across her chest, chin up. "As a matter of fact no, I don't know that. I'm pretty sure Xerxes would make me an offer, too."

"I'm sure he would. But if you switch sides, can you imagine living in a world of death and ashes?" I look to the window, to the colorful spring landscape outside. "All this would wilt and die, turn into black earth and ash. The human world, it would become a hell on Earth, and all the other realms would fall one by one. You know that."

"Xerxes is strong, and has secret allies we know nothing about. Powerful allies. He might win anyway, if the rumors are true about the aces in his sleeve."

I lower my voice. "Zillard has shown Arielle a secret weapon with which we can take Xerxes down. It won't be easy to get it, but we hold the advantage."

It's a huge deal, but Minerva isn't thinking with her usual cold head right now.

"Lysander, you pledged yourself to me, we had a huge engagement ceremony to which we invited all the noble families and clans of the supernatural worlds. You promised to marry me, and make me your bonded mate. I will hold you to that promise. You will give yourself to me, Lysander, or I will take all my military and diplomatic arsenal to Xerxes. And no, I don't care if the world turns to ashes. All this?" She motions to the arched windows that open to the sunny spring outside. "Doesn't matter to me if I can't have you."

Now it dawns on me what changed in the past few months. It was her feelings.

"Minerva, what you feel is obsession. This is sick. I just told you I was in love with another woman, how can you still want me? You're a beautiful, powerful High Fae—"

"I will have her killed, Lysander, if you leave me," she cuts me off. "Keep that in mind when you make your decision."

She looks down from my face to my naked torso, her eyes stopping on the contour of my cock through the fabric of my pants. She touches my waistband, but I step back.

"No," I say dryly. She grins a sick grin.

"Oh, yes you will, if want what's best for your love the water nymph. I'm only willing to wait until the wedding, not a day longer."

"There won't be a wedding, not until after the war. It would be an offense, to our people and our allies, if we put our attention on that while open war is upon us."

"True. But think about it, Lysander Nightfrost," she hisses as she retreats towards the door. "You won't be able to escape this forever. You will comply and take me as your wife. And when you do, you will make me your bonded mate. That should solve your little love problem. You'll forget Arielle de Saelaria as if she'd only been a ghost in the night." She laughs like a lunatic as she reaches the door, gliding out of my chamber, and leaving me with rage in my chest.

She mustn't find out that Arielle is already my bonded mate, or she'll have her killed without a second thought. Arielle is no match for Minerva, not yet. Minerva is resourceful, vicious, and has entire armies at her disposal. And she's losing her mind.

TO BE CONTINUED WITH
THE ICE KING'S SECRET
FEBRUARY 2020

STAY TUNED BY FOLLOWING ANA CALIN ON AMAZON, OR CHECK OUT MORE AT ANA CALIN COMPLETE WORKS

MAGNIFICENT
BEASTS
AVAILABLE ON AMAZON
CLAIMED
BY DRAGO WOLF
ANA CALIN
TAKEN
BY NERO WOLF
ANA CALIN
ANA CALIN
BECOMING THE
RED
WITCH
MAJOR ARCANA ACADEMY

Printed in Great Britain
by Amazon